MW01232654

Chapter 1

A buzzing phone woke Lexi at six in the morning. Her normal wake-up call was from Jake, but since he'd left for California on a late flight the night before, it couldn't be him, could it? She turned over, grabbed the phone from her nightstand and squinted to see the name. She punched the button to answer. "Jake Donovan, what are you doing?"

"Good morning to you too, beautiful."

"Good morning, Jake. It's two in the morning in San Francisco, why are you up and calling me?"

"Long story. Our flight was delayed and the hotel released our rooms so we had to scramble to find a place to stay."

"Wow, what a horrible way to start the trip. Isn't your meeting in a couple of hours?"

"Yeah. Is anything going on there?"

Lexi giggled. "You just left last night. There hasn't been any time for anything to be going on yet."

"Yeah, but I know how trouble can find you, even in the middle of the night. I just wanted to say I'm sorry I'm going to miss your... what did they call it?"

"They call it a marriage gathering. You'd miss it anyway. Only girls are allowed."

"What's it supposed to do?"

"I don't think it's supposed to *do* anything, and I don't really understand it myself. It's some old tradition where all the ladies get together and present items to the upcoming bride. That whole something old, something new thing that brides used to get into."

"I don't get any of that. Sounds more like a reason for them to get together and gossip."

A soft chuckle escaped Lexi. "These ladies don't need a reason to gossip. It's what they do. Anyway, it's an old-time tradition. Most people don't follow it at all anymore, but you know Grams and her friends like to keep things old fashioned. Sometimes I'm surprised they even use telephones, and a computer is almost out of the question."

"But they are charming and it's kind of neat that Cryptic Cove isn't modern like other places. I think that's part of the appeal, along with a very beautiful woman who lives there and will soon be my wife."

"Aww, that's sweet. I should probably get downstairs to help Grams with the party preparations. And you need to get some rest."

"I know, but I wanted to hear your voice. I miss you already."

"I miss you too."

"I should be back within two days. Try to stay out of trouble until then." Jake said with a chuckle.

Lexi's face pinched up, "I will do my best, but you know good and well that trouble finds me. I don't go looking for it."

"I know, but I like it when you squint your eyes and crinkle your nose at me."

"I didn't crinkle my nose."

"You did. Stop denying it."

Guilty. "Okay, I did. Are you happy now."

"I am, but I'll be happier when you're my wife."

Lexi lay in bed a few more minutes, still holding the phone to her chest. She couldn't remember a time since childhood that she'd been happier. Jake took the time to really know her. Sometimes that was scary, but it was also comforting to know that someone loved her enough to pay attention to all her little quirks, and even found them amusing. She figured she'd drive him nuts before their ten year anniversary, but she'd worry about that then. The wedding date was still pending after months of being engaged, but Jake wanted to have everything ready, in case they decided to seize the moment. She secretly thought he was up to something, but she could never prove it.

Other than the daily gossip train, life in Cryptic Cove was pleasantly quiet and relaxing. She stretched again and rolled out of bed to head to the shower. The town's gossipers would expect her to be in the office by eight forty-five, although she arrived by eight thirty to relax with a cup of coffee and prepare herself. If they ever found out, they'd start calling earlier.

She placed the cell phone on the nightstand as an uneasy feeling crept over her. *Life could be too good.* Nothing major had happened, but every time she got quiet and let her mind wander or thought about the future, these feelings started creeping in. She chalked it up to wedding jitters. All brides-to-be got these antsy feelings. Nerves, that's all it was.

* * *

Grams was busy in the kitchen getting cookies and other treats baked when Lexi walked in. A hint of tension was present in the room. Grams was always cheerful, so Lexi could tell something was wrong. She poured herself a cup of coffee and sat down at the small island in the center of the kitchen—Grams' workstation, as she called it, a giant block of wood on four legs where she did all her prep work for cooking and baking.

"Morning, Grams."

Grams stopped long enough from pulling a batch of cookies out of the oven to look at Lexi, "Morning dear. Sleep well?"

"I did, but I get the feeling something is bothering you. Do you want to talk about it?"

Grams placed the cookies on a cooling rack, removed the oven mitt and wiped her hands on her apron before grabbing more eggs to make another batch of cookies. "Oh, it's nothing." She looked up at the small opening over the doorway where Baxter perched every morning while she cooked breakfast. The spot was empty. A look of concern crossed her face before she turned to Lexi and let out a short, exasperated breath. "I'm just a little upset about the way the Historical Society meeting went last night."

"What happened?" Lexi asked as she reached over and grabbed one of the hot cookies from the rack. She blew on it to cool it more quickly before taking a bite.

Grams cracked an egg into the glass mixing bowl. "Everyone is in an uproar about new changes, moving to computer systems and the way some things are being run since new people have taken over. Mavis Clark was throwing accusations at Decatur Williams about the library. Decatur was harping on about Shirley and how Shirley is always a nosey busy-body and keeping everyone in town mad about something or other. Ms. Jensen was trying to keep the peace with everyone. It was just a mess."

Lexi sipped her coffee to wash down the cookie. "It seems Mrs. Williams might have gotten Mavis and Shirley mixed up. Mavis is usually the one keeping things stirred up."

Grams shook her head, probably remembering the time she was on the end of accusations from Mavis when a local couple was murdered right after Lexi moved back to her hometown of Cryptic Cove. It was a time everyone wanted to forget, and luckily, Mavis and Grams had made their peace since then. She finally spoke, "It was odd. Shirley had been a little bit vocal with her thoughts, which is odd for her, she usually shares things in private instead of group meetings. And let's not forget about that reporter. We allowed him into the meeting, and he stirred as much trouble as he could. I thought him and Dale were going to get into a fist fight."

"Mr. Chimay? He's usually so nice."

"Yes usually, but he's gotten a little cantankerous since his retirement and he's more against all of this digital stuff than anyone else. With

All Hallow's Eve coming up, people around here just get a little on edge about the smallest things."

"I agree, it's odd, Grams. I haven't figured out why it bothers the people so much. I mean, they all join in the festivities, but they all act scared that something bad is going to happen, like some curse is going to swoop in and land on the town."

Grams stopped mixing the ingredients she'd added to the bowl and stared off into space, a faraway look in her eyes.

"Grams, what's wrong?"

She started stirring the stuff in the bowl harder than was necessary. "Nothing, child. Just old memories, I suppose. No cause for you to worry."

"What can I do to help?"

Grams' face pinched up as she thought about it. "Can you start loading things into my car? I think I have everything in here under control."

"Sure," Lexi said, grabbing the bag of party supplies to take to Crystal Scents, the candle shop Grams owned. She was concerned about her grandmother's reaction when she joked about a curse. She hadn't meant anything by it, and Grams had blown it off, but it had bothered her more than she wanted to admit. As she loaded the supplies into Grams' car, she thought about the big city reporter in town snooping around and doing an article on Halloween in this town. She couldn't help but think about a forgotten curse. *Was there a curse on this town?* She didn't believe in real curses, but someone could keep the possibility of one alive. That could explain all of the strange behavior and happenings around this time of year. A Halloween curse, even a fake one, was all she needed right now.

Chapter 2

Lexi arrived at the office a few minutes early, hoping to settle in with a cup of coffee before the morning barrage of gossipers called to cue her in on the latest fiascoes with neighbors, chickens, goats or whatever. John had arrived early, so she hollered into his office that she was there as she popped a pod into the coffee machine.

Her boss, John Ballard, town constable of Cryptic Cove, came out of his office. "Make that a to-go cup. There's been some vandalism at the cemetery we need to go check out."

She was only a secretary, but always helped him solve town capers and disputes among the town's folks. She also doubled as the crime scene photographer when necessary.

She placed an insulated thermos cup on the machine and pushed the button. "Who vandalizes cemeteries? That's so tacky."

"It is. We usually get some every year around this time, but the caretaker said this was a bit strange, so we better check it out."

"People do get a little mischievous around Halloween."

"You were new here last year, so you probably didn't notice how strange things can get. The older generation takes this time of year very seriously."

"Some of them take everything seriously, John. I've noticed that."

"Yes, but this is different." John said as he headed to the door. "Let's get this over with."

She grabbed her coffee mug and placed the lid on top. Her camera bag was still hanging on her shoulder, so she headed straight out the door with John and locked up.

The morning air was crisp and a thick fog hovered over the cemetery. At one time, Lexi would have found it creepy, but these days, she often found it rather comforting. Unfortunately, she didn't feel comforted today. As John parked his truck, a little ripple pulsed through her body. She could barely see the area where the mausoleums stood. Something was wrong, but she couldn't pinpoint it. The caretaker was waiting as John got out of the truck and pointed to the tomb that had been desecrated. It was next to the wood line. Lexi stared for a minute more before opening her door and joining John and the caretaker, who were already halfway to the trees. The morning dew sloshed under her feet as she walked quickly to catch up. The niggle in her gut grew stronger with each step closer to the tomb.

She stood in front of the tomb with John. Someone had broken a gargoyle from its pedestal next to the door. Lexi looked down as one eye of the gargoyle looked up at her. She thought she heard whispers. Suddenly, the sky around them filled with crows swooping in and landing in the tree branches and any other surface they could perch on. Lexi looked over towards the trees and saw a burned circle. She walked over and inspected it. A scorched crow lay in the middle of the circle. Shivers shot through her. "John, you need to see this!"

He walked over and looked down. "Oh no. It isn't Baxter is it?"

Lexi turned away for a moment, her heart pinching in her chest. "No. Baxter wears a little tag on his foot. This bird doesn't have one."

"Unless it was removed by someone." John said the words slowly, almost under his breath.

Lexi looked down and let her breath out. "I doubt it. Baxter is pretty picky about who he lets close to him."

"What if he was trapped?"

Lexi shook her head. "I don't think so. He's pretty smart, and crows communicate with one another. This may be a young crow who was easily tricked."

"You know a lot about crows."

"Well, since Baxter took to me so well, I've done some studying. I never knew how amazing they are. They're quite brilliant, actually." She looked around in the trees, "You see how they've all come to this spot."

John looked all around. "Fascinating. I don't think I've ever seen anything like it."

Lexi looked towards the tomb. "Do you think this is related to the vandalism?"

John rubbed his chin. "It's hard to say. I'm sure it's just some kids and their pranks, although we've never had any meanness like this in all the years I've been constable."

"Have any new kids moved into the area?"

"Not that I'm aware of. But one of the local kids could have seen something on one of those horror films and decided to mimic it."

An ill feeling washed over Lexi. "You're probably right, but my gut tells me there's more to it."

John and Lexi walked through the cemetery looking for more signs of vandalism. They discovered a few more burned areas, but none of them contained animals. Some had burned plastic flowers, which had been ripped from grave sites.

They returned to the broken gargoyle. Lexi looked up at the tomb. Vines had grown over the namesake so she stepped up and began pulling them back. A jolt seared through her body when she recognized the name etched into the marble. Danforth. She let out a gasp. John looked up to see what had her so troubled. His mouth gaped open.

Chapter 3

Lexi squinted driving out to Hayden's Ridge in the morning sun. Her grandmother's friend, Shirley, wanted her to stop by and look at an item she thought was perfect for the something old *and* the something blue parts of her wedding attire, but she didn't want to wait until the party that afternoon to show it to Lexi. A smile crossed her face thinking about how close it was getting. It had been over six months since Jake had proposed and they both wanted a fall wedding. With All Hallow's Eve just around the corner, so was the wedding. At least she assumed it was just around the corner. They hadn't actually set a date.

Lexi drew in a deep breath. The cool fall air filled her nose with the smell of cedar and pine. She looked at her watch, noting she was a bit early, but the caterer had called and needed her back in town before noon to work out some details of the menu.

Hayden's Ridge was the retirement village located just outside of town on the edge of a cliff overlooking the ocean. The cottages were charming and perfect for older people who weren't quite ready for the nursing home that was also on the property. This allowed people their freedom, but gave them added security knowing a doctor or nurse was close by if they required any assistance.

Lexi walked towards Shirley's cottage. A rush of cold air swirled around her, giving her a chill and an uneasy feeling. As she approached the door, she noticed it was slightly open. Since the elderly lady was expecting her, she figured she'd left the door open and intended for Lexi to come on in. It was almost a tradition in Cryptic Cove.

Lexi pushed the door open and peeked into the room, "Shirley? It's Lexi, I'm a little bit early."

She gasped when movement caught her eye. A hooded figure ran out the patio door. She ran in hoping to get a better look at the person before they disappeared.

"Shirley, someone is in your house, are you okay?" She yelled as she looked out the patio door. Whoever had been in Shirley's home had already vanished into the wooded area.

Lexi turned, the smell of burned cloth seeped into her nostrils. A light fog of smoke drifted in from the other room. Beams of sunlight highlighted the small wisps floating around the room.

"Fire!" She yelled as she called out to Shirley again. "I think something is burning. We need to find out what it is."

She looked towards the open door where the smoke came from. She entered the bedroom and saw a dark mass on the floor, smoldering, the smoke thicker in this room. Her hands went to her chest realizing what she was looking at.

She hurried to the mass and looked down. "Oh no!" She shrieked.

Heavy sobs escaped her as tears streamed down her face upon seeing the body of Shirley on the floor. She sucked in a deep breath and tried to gain some kind of composure. She looked around the room, but didn't see any candles nearby, only a smashed jewelry box lying on the floor, jewelry scattered everywhere. Apparently she'd interrupted a robbery, but why would anyone use such a cruel method to get a handful of jewelry?

She looked back at the body on the floor. Tears continued to stream down her face. She'd found her share of bodies since moving back to Cryptic Cove, but this was the most disturbing. This lady had been a long-time friend of her grandmother's. How would the town be able to handle this?

She composed herself and pulled out her cellphone to call John.

The sheriff arrived shortly after John. Of course he started giving her the third degree for being the one to find another body in Cryptic Cove.

Lexi stood straight and crossed her arms over her chest. "Why do you always assume it has something to do with me?"

"Miss Danforth, you've only been here a little over a year and a half. This is the fourth murder in that time. This town hadn't had a murder in over ten years when you came back. How do you think that looks? Besides, you have this strange habit of finding the bodies."

"That's ludicrous. I can't help that I find the bodies, but I assure you, I've had nothing to do with any of these deaths. You know good and well that I've always helped with these investigations and been more than cooperative."

"Humphhh. I'm still keeping my eye on you."

"Of course you are. I wouldn't expect anything less." Lexi turned and headed out the door. The overbearing sheriff was the least of her problems at the moment. She wanted to get to her grandmother before the town gossip train took off. Grams would take the news much better if it came from her. She only hoped she was alone at Crystal Scents, although she knew there was a slim chance of that. She made a quick phone call to Peyton while she drove the short trip back into town. She knew Peyton would keep it quiet until a statement was released to the public.

Grams and Ms. Jensen took the news more calmly than Lexi expected. She stared at them in disbelief as they shot each other sideways glances.

Did they know something? She didn't want to seem overly suspicious of the two older women, but their behavior was strange indeed.

They were almost unemotional at the news. Maybe they were in shock. Grams looked over at Ms. Jensen after a few quiet moments. Ms. Jensen returned the look, her face slightly pinched, like she was using some kind of ESP to speak with her eyes. Grams raised an eyebrow. Neither woman was wailing or crying at the loss of their friend. Was there something more to this? Something Lexi was missing? Surely they weren't speaking to each other without using words. They were just in shock and unsure of how they should react in front of each other. A tear trickled down Grams face, the first sign of any real emotion. Lexi felt the sadness surround them, but that didn't explain why they were being so out of sorts about the whole thing. Baxter flew in from the backroom. Grams had a small doorway built for him over the backdoor so he could come and go as he pleased, just like at her home. He landed on Grams' shoulder and appeared to whisper in her ear. Her face turned pale as she looked at Ms. Jensen again, this time her expression more ominous. Lexi didn't know what was going on, but it was strange, more strange than she'd seen these two women act before, and she had seen some strange things the past year and a half. There was definitely a new murder case in Cryptic Cove, but what did it mean? The whole thing reeked of a cult or something. Lexi wasn't sure she was up for this one, but she and John had to get to the bottom of it.

Chapter 4

The day had been long, mentally and emotionally draining. Lexi tucked herself into bed and stared at the ceiling. The nightlight from the hallway cast shadows throughout the room, but the ceiling appeared to glow at times. She and John had more questions than answers and nothing pieced together. The idea that they were working on several cases instead of just two crossed her mind. Nothing made sense. They even considered the fact that they were trying to put pieces into the wrong puzzle. Perhaps they were grasping at straws.

Her droopy eyelids grew heavy and she drifted off to sleep.

"Stop them!" The voice was clear. Her eyes flew open and she looked around. No one was there. In the darkness she was looking at the mausoleum, the broken gargoyle lying on the ground staring up at her. She shook her head. *How can this be?* The caretaker had already cleared the crime scene and was working on getting the creature restored. Whispers carried across the fog that rolled in and enveloped her. A man's voice, and then another, sliced through the thick moisture. She knew that voice. She strained to listen. "Find the truth. The town has secrets."

She awoke in a cold sweat, like the damp fog had crept into the room and drenched the entire bed. She sat up and looked around. It had only been a dream, but it felt so real. *Or was it a dream?* She and John had run so many scenarios around that day it was possible her subconscious mind was overwhelmed and trying to piece anything together that made sense. Of course, standing in a cemetery in the middle of the night listening to voices made absolutely no sense. But this town, and the people, weren't exactly known for making a whole lot of sense. *What did the voice say?* The town has secrets. *Why is the voice so familiar and why can't I place it?*

She got out of bed and headed downstairs for a cup of chamomile tea. Tomorrow would be another trying day and she needed rest. They couldn't ignore the reporter any longer. He would have questions about the murder investigation now, and not just his silly Halloween story. Plus, it was possible he knew something and could be behind the vandalism and the death of Shirley.

Lexi found her Aunt Agatha sitting at the kitchen table, the light over the sink illuminated the room just enough to see her. She walked over to her aunt and placed her hand on her aunt's shoulder as she noticed another cup of tea sitting on the opposite side of the table. "Are you and Grams having trouble sleeping too?" She asked as she pointed to the steamy cup.

"That's for you."

Her eyes grew wide. "How did you know I was coming down for a cup of tea."

Agatha waved her hand in the air, nonchalantly. "You and Velda aren't the only ones with the intuition thing." She said with a smile.

Lexi sat down in the chair across from her and took a sip. "Can you tell me about this so-called gift we have? It's not doing me a lot of good right now. It won't even tell me who killed Shirley, why they killed her and how all these pieces fit together."

"The town likes to keep its secrets."

Lexi almost choked on the tea. "What did you say?"

"Secrets. The town likes to keep them."

She stared at Agatha in disbelief. Her aunt knew all about secrets. She had been one of the best kept secrets in this town for most of her adult life.

Agatha cocked her head sideways, "You look like you've seen a ghost or something. What's wrong Lexi?"

"A voice in my dream. It said the same thing, that the town has secrets."

"Then you should start digging into that."

"What do you know, Aunt Agatha?" She leaned forward and raised her eyebrows. "You've lived here all your life."

Agatha put her cup down. "Well, for twenty-five of those years I wasn't exactly an active part of this town."

"I know, I just thought maybe you remembered something from your childhood."

"We buried something." Her aunt said, just above a whisper.

"Really? Do you remember where? Maybe we could go dig it up."

"No, sweetie, not like something in the ground. At least I don't think it was something literal that they buried. I seem to remember it was our grandparents. I heard voices in the living room one night, so I snuck downstairs. Several of the town's people were here. I heard them saying the secrets needed to be buried and never mentioned again. I remember trying to get Velda and Shirley to help me go dig for the treasure. At the time, I thought they had really buried a treasure."

"What if they did? What if that's what all of this is about? People kill for things like that all the time."

Agatha's forehead creased, "I'm not so sure. As we got older and asked about it, our parents told us it was simply secrets that needed to stay buried."

"But, they may have said that to keep you from digging up buried treasure."

"True." She grew quiet like her thoughts were wandering. "Have you tried the library?"

"I plan on going there tomorrow."

"Ms. Jensen was librarian for over 40 years. Maybe you should ask her too," Agatha said as she stood up. She walked around the table and kissed Lexi on the forehead. "You'll find the answers. I have no doubt. You found me, remember?"

Lexi finished the tea and headed back upstairs to bed with still more questions, but oddly, she felt better about the fact that this town did have secrets from long ago. Maybe the dreams were kind of like premonitions, although they didn't really tell her anything.

Chapter 5

Lexi met Peyton for a late lunch and told her about the vandalism at the cemetery, the crow that appeared to be sacrificed and how Shirley had been murdered in a similar fashion. Peyton said it sounded like something from a cult movie. And they both agreed the way Grams and Ms. Jensen handled the news was quite odd, even for them.

"Of course, they are very stoic women," Peyton said. "Perhaps, with all the murders here the past year and a half, they've become desensitized to it?"

"You could be right, but Shirley was a long-time friend. How can that not send them into an emotional state? The more I think about it, the more it seems like they were expecting something bad to happen."

"What do you mean?" Peyton asked.

"I'm not sure, but the initial expression on their faces was shock, but then it turned into dread, like they realized something bad had been coming or something."

Peyton tapped her fingers on the table. "I know there's some pretty old town secrets. I barely remember them being mentioned when I was a kid, but the whole town has gone quiet about the past."

"Maybe it's related to the past then." Lexi suggested.

"This has always been a strange town and my parents never would tell me the history. I've gone to the library, but all the information on older town history doesn't exist. It only goes back so far."

"Really? Most libraries keep all of the town historical documents and newspapers."

"This one doesn't. In fact, I asked Ms. Jensen when she was the librarian, and she claimed there had been a fire that destroyed everything."

"Maybe that's true?" Lexi inquired.

"I don't think so. This town has never mentioned a big fire at the library. It seems something of that magnitude would still be talked about today."

"You're right. Somehow we're going to have to dig into this and find out the truth. A good place to start is with Grams and Ms. Jensen, but I have a feeling they aren't going to be very forthcoming with any information."

"You're probably right about that."

"Although, John has been here just as long. I think I'll start by questioning him. He's never kept anything from me before. If he knows anything I'm sure he'll tell me."

"I hope so. A case like this is going to turn the town completely upside down. It's going to be a lot worse than the last two murder cases you and John worked on."

"That's what I'm afraid of." Lexi let out a sigh, the corners of her mouth turning downward.

"Oh, didn't you mention a historical society meeting the other day?"

"I did, and Grams came home pretty upset. I think that meeting may be connected to Shirley's death and that old mausoleum at the cemetery. The crazy thing is, the name on the old tomb is my last name."

"Are you serious? I didn't think any Danforth's had been here before your dad moved here to marry your mom."

"I didn't either, but it seems there was. I was going to go to the library, but after what you just told me, I doubt I'll find much information about it."

"It sounds like something else for which our town elders may be the best resource we can tap into."

"I agree." Lexi said as she jotted something in her a notepad.

"Do you think this is going to affect the wedding?"

Lexi's heart sank at the mention of her upcoming wedding. "Without an official date set, it's hard to tell. I guess it depends on how long this drags out. It doesn't seem like the right time for a celebration."

"We'll get to the bottom of this." She patted Lexi's hand. "You know you can count on me to be as nosy as I can without seeming too obvious."

Lexi reached over and pulled Peyton into a hug. "I should get back to the office. I'm sure John has turned the ringer off on the phone by now, so he can get some work done, or the reporter has barged in wanting to know why our meeting was canceled."

* * *

Lexi paused as she entered the constable's office. Her eyes scanned the room. Nothing was out of place, but an ominous feeling swept over her. The same feeling she'd had when she walked into Shirley's place earlier. She'd gotten used to having some kind of sixth sense about little things, and an occasional gut feeling when it came to solving cases, but this was more than that. This sucked the breath out of her, like someone had punched her in the chest. She drew in a deep breath and composed herself as she walked over to the door of John's office and peeked in. He was sitting in his chair staring at something on his desk. She tapped on the door frame to get his attention.

With a ragged breath he spoke, "Come in Lexi. I want you to see this."

She walked over and looked down at the object that had him so mesmerized. It was a cylindrical device with lettering on it and things that looked like tumblers in a lock. She had seen similar items in movies. Small items that could hold small bits of paper or jewelry. The uneasy feeling washed over her again as she stared at the item. After a few minutes she shook her head. *Why was this thing so intriguing?* She looked at John. "What is it, exactly?"

"I believe it's a Cryptex. Very much like a combination lock, except these will open and reveal a compartment inside."

"Where did you get it?"

John rubbed his eyes before looking up at her. "It was clutched in Shirley's hand."

"Oh my gosh! I wonder why she was holding that?"

"I think it contains secrets this town buried long ago. I'm guessing Shirley was the keeper."

"The what?" John wasn't making much sense, but this was a good opportunity to question him about the town's past. Agatha and Peyton had mentioned that the whole town stopped speaking of things many years ago. Lexi searched her memories trying to remember back to her childhood, before her father packed up and moved to the city. She would almost get a glimpse of something, but it would fade quickly.

John used a pencil to turn the object around on his desk, afraid to touch it. He took in a deep breath. "It hasn't been mentioned in many years, but there's always been someone designated as a keeper in this town, someone who keeps up with the town's past and has hidden much of Cryptic Cove's secrets. It's been so long it's become a fairy tale of sorts. It hasn't been mentioned since I was a child."

Lexi sat down in the chair. "Aunt Agatha remembers their grandparents hiding something. Maybe that thing is what they were hiding." Lexi said as she pointed at the object. "And Peyton vaguely remembers her parents talking about the town going silent when we were kids, but she can't remember anything else. I was going to ask you about it before I start digging into some research on the Danforth name inscribed on that tomb."

John looked up at Lexi. "I still need to run down some leads on the fires and the vandalism at the cemetery."

"Do you think the two are linked?"

For the first time since she'd met John, she saw fear in his eyes. His hands trembled as he grabbed a handkerchief and wrapped it around the item before shoving it into the inside pocket of his jacket. "I don't know." The words stuttered out of his mouth. "I, um, I have some things to do. Keep an eye on the office." And just like that, he was out the door.

Lexi didn't want to close the office completely, it was too early, so going to the library was out of the question today. But, she'd kept some of the paid research sites in good standing, so she decided to see if there was any kind of information about the Danforth who'd lived here. She pulled out her cellphone, looked at the picture she had taken and decided to start with the dates under the name.

Two hours later, she had found very little information at all. It's like the person, and even this town, had never existed. She checked the clock as she leaned back in her chair. John had been gone awhile, which wasn't all that strange, but she was starting to get a little worried. She closed her eyes and hoped

Jake would call during his lunch break on the west coast.

Her cell phone buzzed, jerking her back into reality. *Had Jake read her mind and decided to call?* She looked at the screen before pushing the answer button. "John, are you okay?"

"Someone broke into the morgue while Marcus was gone to get something to eat. I need you to come down here. Bring your camera." The line went dead. Lexi grabbed her things, turned on the answering machine and locked the office. The morgue was only a few blocks over. It was just as fast to walk the short distance as it was to go get her car from the parking lot behind the building, so she took off towards the morgue on foot.

Chapter 6

Checking out the morgue didn't take long, and soon John and Lexi were headed back to the office. John pulled his truck into the alley behind their office and parked close to the back door. He got out of the truck, but stopped halfway to the door and put up his hand. He glanced over his shoulder at Lexi. "The backdoor is open. You stay out here while I go inside and check it out."

A few minutes passed before John stuck his head out. "It's clear," he said as he put his gun away. "But there's a big mess in here."

Lexi had pulled out her taser to zap anyone if they came out the door. She put it away and followed John into the building. The place was ransacked, file drawers pulled out, the contents dumped on the floor. Every file cabinet and every desk drawer had been rifled through. "They were looking for something. Probably the same something they were looking for at the morgue."

John rubbed his chin. "I believe so, too."

"You left here with the Cryptex earlier. Where is it?"

He looked at Lexi with concern in his eyes. "Don't you worry. It's safe."

"Someone wants it pretty bad to go through all this trouble and to kill someone for it."

"I know." The words came out quietly.

"Did you manage to open the thing to see what's inside?"

"No. I didn't want to even try. I've heard tales of things like that being booby-trapped. It could contain a cyanide pill or something."

"I doubt someone would go to all the trouble of keeping it secret all these years if it only contained a poisoned pill. There has to be more to it."

"You're probably right, especially after all the vandalism and break-ins we've had surrounding the item. But, how would anyone but Shirley know about it now?"

"That's a good question, and I'm not so sure the answer will be easy to find."

John called and reported both break-ins to the sheriff. It took about an hour to get everything back in place. Lexi informed John she was headed to the library before it closed for the day. She wanted to see if she could dig up any old records on the town's history.

Being the oldest building in town, the library was also the most elaborate, full of beautiful architecture and an old world charm. The people who built the town must have believed in education and history, because they went to such an extreme to make the library stand out. Most towns have the courthouse in the center of town, but in Cryptic Cove, it's the library that's located there. Lexi found it odd that the settlers put so much emphasis on a place of history, but then later generations went to so much trouble to bury history. She also didn't understand why she'd been told the original building had burned. Maybe it had, and they'd replaced it with this more elaborate one.

She looked around some of the archives that were available in the main part of the library, but didn't find anything. She didn't look forward to speaking to Decatur Williams, the librarian, to ask for the older files, but knew there was no other choice. The woman could be snooty, and from what Lexi had been told by her Grams, she got very defensive about the past. *Perhaps she knows some things are better left in the past and covered up.* Whoever else was digging into the past sure had opened a can of worms over it and gone as far as to commit murder. It couldn't be good. Lexi walked over to the counter to speak to Mrs. Williams and tried to make small talk, mentioning the weather.

The lady's eyebrows pinched together as she stared down her nose at Lexi. "Shouldn't you be trying to find the murderer in this town instead of asking me about the weather?"

"Yes, ma'am. That's why I'm here actually. I need to find out some information about the town's past?"

"What does that have to do with Shirley being," her bottom lip quivered, "murdered?"

"Other clues indicate it may have something to do with the past."

"If I remember correctly, she was a wild one back in her day. At least that's what my late husband said about her. There's no telling who she offended or what she got off into."

"Well, it seems to revolve around the town itself."

"Really? That's strange. This has always been such a quiet little town." She looked down her nose again, over the small framed glasses, "At least until you showed back up. Things have gotten a little out of hand since then, haven't they?"

"Excuse me? What are you implying?" Lexi asked.

"Implying? Nothing, but it is a bit obvious that murders started happening upon your return." She looked down and checked her watch. "The library is closing now. I'm sure I can't help you anyway. The town records only go back so far and nothing weird is mentioned in them."

"And you've read through all of the records?"

"I am the librarian. It's my job to know what's in the library and the town history." She checked her watch again.

Lexi noticed a bandage on her hand and started to ask about it, but she was already being so rude, she didn't want to bother with any more small talk.

Lexi left the library with more questions than she had answers for. If the librarian was supposed to know the town history, then she'd have to speak to Ms. Jensen, as she was the previous librarian. It wouldn't hurt to speak to Mavis Clark either. She was in charge of a lot of the town's records. That wasn't an interview Lexi looked forward to. She had gotten a little nicer over the past year, but she hadn't become a pleasant woman, not by any stretch of the word.

There was nothing more she could do today. She got in her car and headed home.

Chapter 7

The next morning Lexi stopped at Peyton's B&B to grab some pastries before heading to her Grams' shop. Each lady had a day to bring treats for morning gossip, and today was her day. She loaded the tasty goodies into her car and headed into town.

When she stepped inside Crystal Scents, a buzz in the air tickled her senses. The ladies were in full gossip mode and evidently upset about something. She pulled the pastries out of the bag and placed them on a plate before heading to the coffee machine Grams' had installed for her customers.

Grams' face was pinched when she looked up at her. "Have you spoken to that reporter yet?"

Lexi sat down on a stool behind the counter. All eyes were on her, waiting for an answer.

"No. We're scheduled to meet him later this afternoon. What's wrong?"

Mavis Clark was the first to speak. "He's digging his nose in where it doesn't belong."

Mavis had a way with drama and keeping things stirred up in town. But, Lexi had learned to appease her by pretending to be interested in what she had to say. "Oh, from what we were told, he's doing a Halloween story, so he would dig into old traditions and such."

Mavis rolled her eyes. "He's asking about more than Halloween traditions. He's asking about early settlers and how this town began."

"What's wrong with that?"

Mavis crossed her arms over her chest and looked down her nose at Lexi.

Ms. Jensen cleared her throat, seeing that Mavis was clearly upset. "Well, we don't like people snooping around about our past. We've always been a tight-knit little town and we don't take kindly to outsiders coming in here and stirring things up."

Lexi knew that all too well. When she returned here after being raised in the city, it had been a while before many of the people warmed up to her. If they hadn't known her as a child or that she was Velda's granddaughter, it's likely they never would have accepted her. They welcomed tourists, but not those who came here and planned to stay. She looked around at the group of ladies staring at her. "I'll find out what he's fishing for and why he's being so nosy."

"He's also asking us about Shirley's death," Ms. Jensen replied, "Maybe you should ask him why he's so interested in that too."

"I will. I promise. But that is a news story and reporters are interested in the news, especially when it's something as bizarre as her death."

"Murder," Mavis Clark said, looking at her. "It was murder. You know it, I know it. The whole town knows it. I'm not so sure he didn't have something to do with it."

"He didn't even know Shirley. Why would he kill her?"

"For a better story than some silly Halloween traditions."

The bells over the door jingled. Everyone turned to see Decatur Williams hurrying through the door. She headed straight to where Grams was standing. "I'm running late this morning," she said as she placed a stack of books on the counter in front of

Grams. "That silly cat got out this morning. I spent an hour chasing that thing down, and I have to get to the library early to start pulling some older books about Halloween for that incessant reporter in town." She patted the books she'd placed on the counter and never lost a beat, "These are the books you asked me about the other day. It took a while to gather them all up. It seems some of them were mis-categorized," she stressed the last word as she cut her eyes towards Ms. Jensen. "The place is a complete mess in some sections."

Grams looked from Ms. Jensen back to Decatur. "Oh dear, Decatur, what happened to your hand?" she asked, pointing to the bandage on the woman's hand.

Decatur rubbed the bandaged hand with her good hand and stood silent for a moment before returning to her bantering speech. "That silly cat. He was so excited about his escape and making me chase him down. When I finally caught him, he latched onto me with his claws and his teeth. Clearly he did not want to be captured." She said with a slight giggle.

"You should have that checked by a doctor."

Decatur waved her other hand in the air, "No time. Busy, busy. I'm sure it'll be okay. I've got to run now, I'll catch you all later."

And like a whirlwind she was gone as fast as she'd appeared. The woman was known to be a talker, but today she was in overdrive. Everyone sat quietly after she left, apparently worn out from the way the woman had rushed in, talked a blue streak and left.

Chapter 8

By the time the ladies were done with their morning vigil, Lexi had an hour left before having to head to the constable's office. A dozen or so questions ran through her head, so she headed back to the B&B to run some things by Peyton.

"The ladies were clearly upset over the reporter snooping around. They're wondering why he's so interested in Shirley's death and the town's past."

"He *is* a reporter, and granted, that story is a lot more interesting than the one he came here to write about old Halloween traditions."

"That's what I told them, but they weren't happy with that explanation. Of course, Decatur Williams came in like a whirlwind chatting ninety to nothing and she seemed to be okay with having to meet him. The tension between her and Ms. Jensen was thick."

"Is it that obvious?"

"It was more of a feeling, but as Ms. Williams was explaining to Grams that she had trouble finding the books Grams requested, she cut her eyes at Ms. Jensen about how books had been categorized in the library."

"There may be some animosity there," Peyton said. "What books did your Grams get?"

"I didn't get a chance to ask, and no clue why it was a big deal about them being in the wrong section. I'll have to ask Grams later to straighten that out. Another thing I find odd is that Grams and her friends don't have a lot to do with Ms. Williams."

"It's probably the whole library thing. Ms. Jensen ran the library most of her life and you know how protective the older ones are about their place in this town. I suspect the same thing will happen when someone steps up to take over the Magistrate's Office from Mavis Clark. Sparks will fly when they tell her she's too old to do her job."

"You have a point there. Ms. Williams was clearly hyped up after having to chase her cat all morning."

"She has a cat?" Peyton cocked her head sideways. "I've never known her to mention having any pets."

"Apparently she does and he's pretty feisty. When she finally caught him, he clawed her up pretty good. She had a bandage covering her hand.

"Ah, maybe he's a new cat and he doesn't like her too much," Peyton suggested as she stifled a giggle. "That's not funny, but I really can't imagine a cat liking her. She's always so uppity."

"Well, this morning she was a chatterbox." Lexi paused. "I didn't think about it at the time but she had that bandage on her hand yesterday. Maybe the cat attacks her everyday?"

"That's definitely strange and I can't say I blame the poor kitty."

"That's what I was thinking. I also got the impression she's excited about talking to the reporter, despite the fact that the rest of the ladies are not."

"It's probably nothing. With everything going on, everyone is acting a bit odd. Have you and John found out any more about that item Shirley had in her hands?"

"Not really, but the morgue was broken into and our office too. Both places were ransacked, so we suspect whoever did it is looking for that thing."

"It would have to be someone who knew Shirley and knew that she had it."

"You're right. I didn't really think about that, and that means that half the town may be suspects now."

"Oh boy. That's not going to make things any easier. I know how upset they all got when that elderly couple was murdered and you and John had to dig into that."

Lexi sat quietly, thinking about everything that she didn't have answers for. When she looked up Peyton was staring at her, her eyebrows pinched together. "Sorry, I was thinking about something else."

"I noticed. Wanna share what that was?"

Lexi told her about the voice in her dream the night before, and that she wasn't sure it was a dream or just a voice in her head. "I know strange things happen in this town, but Aunt Agatha repeated the same words to me when I went downstairs for a cup of tea. I'm not fully ready to accept that the dead, or something, are sending me messages. There has to be a logical explanation for it."

"I agree. That's kind of creepy."

"I wish we knew more about that Cryptex. It seems awfully familiar to me, but I don't think I've ever seen one."

"OH," Peyton exclaimed, "There's a movie that came out a long time ago. You and Jake should rent it when he gets back."

"I don't see how a movie would help."

"It may not, but it may help you to think things through from a different angle. I think it was about a code of some sorts. Yeah, the Da Vinci Code."

"I guess it can't hurt. We're definitely clueless as it is. How about we all have a date night and watch it together?"

"I don't think me hanging out with you and Jake is a date."

Lexi giggled, "Don't try to deny that you and Charlie have been hanging out together. A lot! Ask him to come. He's read a lot of books, too, and maybe he knows something about the history of these items."

Peyton pinched her face up. "We're not dating."

"Okay, don't call it a date. It's not like we haven't all hung out together before."

"You're right. It could be interesting. When does Jake get back?"

"Tomorrow, and that's not soon enough for me. I miss him."

Lexi headed to the constable's office, thinking about Jake. He'd only been gone two days, but it seemed like weeks. She felt like she was going in circles with not being able to bounce questions off him. They'd spoken enough on the phone for him to know a little about the situation, but that was it. Peyton and her always brainstormed ideas, but then she'd run them by Jake to get his opinion.

On top of all this, she was supposed to be planning a wedding, but it had taken a backseat to this murder investigation. It didn't look like this one would be solved anytime soon, either. There was still way more to dig into.

Chapter 9

All day long, Lexi had a strange feeling she couldn't shake. She and John discussed what they knew so far, and it wasn't much. Shirley had definitely been killed. She'd had a strange object in her hand. The morgue and their office had both been ransacked, and they could only assume it was because of that strange item. Whoever wanted it wanted it bad enough to take chances in broad daylight.

Lexi looked at John. "Grams and the other ladies are upset with how the reporter is snooping around. I thought they were being silly, but the more I think about it, the more I'm concerned he should be a suspect."

"We can't just suspect him because he's irritating people."

"I know, but back when I worked at the law firm in the city, the reporters could get pretty brave. They were constantly sneaking in and trying to get insider information. If this guy is like those guys were, he'd go to great lengths to get what he wants. If that happens to be that Cryptex thing, we may have a problem with him."

"You may have a point. We're so used to old man Jordon knowing everyone's business without having to snoop around, that we aren't familiar with how a real reporter would act or what they'd do to get a story. I guess we've kept ourselves too sheltered in our little town." John let out a sigh as he sat back in the chair.

"That's completely understandable. Everything and everyone here seems to be set in their ways, and it works out for the whole town."

"If it weren't for tourists, we probably wouldn't even know an outside world existed, to be honest. Maybe that's not a good thing. We don't trust outsiders, which isn't a bad thing, but it could also be the thing that causes us the most trouble. Perhaps we've locked too much away, even from ourselves." John's words trailed off. He wasn't making a lot of sense, but his last statement sparked her curiosity.

"John, do you remember any dark secrets in this town's past that someone would be after?"

He sat in silence for a few long seconds, lines etched across his forehead as he was deep in his thoughts. When he finally looked up at Lexi, his face was contorted, like his mind was grasping for a lost memory. "That's a good question. So much time has passed since childhood, but there was something. Something that rattled our grandparents back then. I think maybe they wanted the past buried. I do remember as kids, we would all try to figure out what the big deal was. Of course, stories of curses led our imaginations all over the place. We eventually forgot all about it though."

"Maybe it's time you and the others start trying to remember, so we can figure this out."

"You're right, but sometimes the lines between myth and legend get blurred. We were so young and our parents were insistent that some things never get mentioned again."

"Well, we need to start jogging your memory, even if you think it's silly, and try to put some pieces together. The library should have old newspapers and documents, but Ms. Williams seems awfully protective of anything like that, and she's not real happy when I ask about it."

The phone rang causing them both to jump a little. John picked it up. The look on his face told Lexi something else was up. He hung up and looked at her. "Speaking of Ms. Williams, that was her. Someone has broken into the library."

"Does she know what's missing?"

"No, says she saw the mess and called us straight away. We better get down there."

Chapter 10

Ms. Williams clutched her chest as John and Lexi approached her, the bandage still visible on her hand from the fiasco with her cat. She recounted how she entered the library, like any other time. She unlocked the door, went inside and began turning lights on. That's when she noticed the door to the backroom was slightly ajar. On her husband's grave, she swore she never leaves it open. When she peeked inside, she noticed files and boxes had been gone through.

John looked around the room, asking her if she noticed anything missing. She replied that she couldn't really tell because she hadn't been through every file herself. That remark piqued Lexi's suspicion. It was the opposite of what she had said to her on a prior visit to the library looking for old files. "Ms. Williams, the other day you told me you'd been through all of the files."

She glared at Lexi for a moment before speaking. "Yes, I have been through all of the files in the main section of the library, not these files."

"So, you lied or you're hiding something?"

"Definitely not!" Her snippy tone bit through the air, "The files you were looking for would have been in the main section. I didn't find it relevant that I haven't been through the files in this room."

She had a point, but Lexi didn't like her attitude. Of course she couldn't let her dislike for someone get in the way of an investigation. Her personal feelings were moot, but her gut was telling her there was something off about the woman's story.

"Right," John broke in, "But it may be relevant now." He said as he looked over his notes. "We all know you close the library to take your lunch. You were late getting back today. Can you tell us where you were?"

"I met with that reporter and then I had errands to run."

"What kind of errands," John asked.

"The personal kind. If you ask me, whoever vandalized the cemetery could have done this.

Apparently, nothing is sacred in this town anymore. Are you doing anything to find out who is going around destroying things?"

"We are looking into it, but a murder investigation takes precedence. I'm sure you're aware of that."

"Yes. I'm sorry. Everything has me on edge lately. I know you have a job to do."

"We'll let you know when we have more information for you. In the meantime, it wouldn't hurt to hire an assistant or have someone stay here with you."

John wanted to believe it was just some kid, or kids, pulling pranks because of Halloween, but this was turning into more than a coincidence of events.

As they headed out of the back room to leave the library, Lexi noticed a small piece of cloth lodged in a splinter on the door. She grabbed the tweezers out of her backpack and a small plastic evidence bag. She didn't know if it was a clue, or how long it had been lodged there, but Marcus Finche would be happy to look at it. As town coroner he'd also taken an interest in forensics. It began as a hobby for him, but over the past two years he'd invested quite a bit of time and money into setting up a small lab. This little fiber would give him something to look into. It probably had nothing to do with their case, but it would be nice if it lead them in a new direction to check out.

Chapter 11

John decided it was time to question Mr. Norman Davis, the reporter who had come into town a few days earlier. Not only did he have the whole town stirred up, but everything weird going on had started after his arrival. He was staying in a little bungalow close to the boardwalk, the real tourist section of Cryptic Cove that was nestled into a small cove on the ocean shore.

The boardwalk was practically empty this time of morning. The colder breeze from the ocean could bite right through you. Store owners and shopkeepers were busy getting ready to open for when the tourists would start emerging from their hotel rooms and wander around looking at the sights. The bungalows were at the far end, tucked into the tree line that surrounded a small beach. The reporter was registered into number nine. It was the most secluded, and probably one Lexi would have chosen if she were a writer and needed to be away from all the noise of the boardwalk.

She raised her hand to knock on the door. John stopped her and pointed to the blood on the doorknob. He pulled out his gun before nodding for Lexi to knock on the door. They listened, but didn't hear anything. Lexi dug around in her bag, pulled out a latex glove and slipped it over her hand so she could try the doorknob to see if it was unlocked. The knob turned easily, but the blood was still damp, probably from all the fog in the air, which would make it impossible to tell how long it had been there. She pushed the door open so John could go inside to check things out while she stayed on the small porch and looked around the area to see if anything else was out of the ordinary. After a few minutes, John called her to come inside. Norman Davis lay on the floor, blood covering his face from a deep gash above his left eye. He'd been conked on the head with something heavy, from the looks of it. Lexi looked around the small room but didn't find anything he could've been hit with.

John looked at her as he pulled out his cell phone. "The sheriff won't be happy about this."

Lexi shook her head in agreement. "Have you noticed we tend to get our murders in sets of two."

"I was trying not to." John said as he walked over to inspect the body while waiting for the sheriff's office to answer. "You better get Marcus out here to take the body into town."

Lexi pulled out her cell phone and called Marcus Finche. He said he'd be there in about half an hour. She relayed the message to John. He nodded as he dug around in the reporter's pockets.

"Here's his car keys." John said as he tossed them to her. "Go see what you can find in it. This room is pretty bare. I don't even see his camera or a laptop."

She left the room thinking how odd it was that none of his equipment was in his room. But then again, it could be smart. People had been known to break into these little bungalows. With any luck he knew his stuff would be safer in his car. If not, then they'd have to consider this a robbery gone bad and not part of the ongoing murder investigation.

She clicked the button, heard the sound of the locks popping up and opened the driver's side door. Typical reporter. He practically lived in his car. Food wrappers, empty coffee cups. It wasn't as bad as she'd seen in the city, but it was still pretty bad. With a gloved hand she moved some trash around, looking to see if a computer or camera was hiding underneath. She found nothing.

Lexi climbed out of the car and walked to the trunk. She was a bit reluctant to pop it open, afraid she'd find a worse mess than the one she just dug through. She inhaled and clicked the trunk release button on the fob. The latch released and the trunk opened a few inches. *Here goes*, she thought, as she pushed the trunk lid open. *Bingo!* The interior of the man's car looked like a slob lived in it, but his trunk was pristine. Everything was neatly organized; file folders, his laptop, his camera and accessories. Lexi let out a sigh of relief. Hopefully she could find some clues in his files or on his computer. Luckily Jake was headed home, so if she needed a hacker to get into the computer files, Jake was the guy. His hacking skills weren't a fact he let everyone know about, but since he'd helped with a few cases that required more computer skills than Lexi had, he'd finally told her about them. Now he hacked away at anything that gave them problems.

Chapter 12

John sent Lexi home early, knowing that Jake would be returning home. He asked if she'd take the files and computer home with her and have Jake start digging into the contents. She knew Jake would want to be updated on everything that had happened the past few days, so she agreed. She couldn't wait to see him, but she also couldn't wait to run some things by him and get his opinion. He was often more objective about things than she was, especially if it involved friends, family or emotions, and so far, this case included all three. It hadn't been mentioned in awhile, but Lexi was still very concerned about the tomb that had been defaced, her last name on the crypt, and how it all tied into Shirley's death.

The one lead and suspect they had was now dead. He couldn't give them any answers. She thought about why someone would kill him. He had been snooping around the town and made enemies of almost everyone. Anyone could have killed him, but the majority of the town's residents were kind, caring people. Of course, the worst could be brought out in people, causing them to do things they wouldn't normally do to protect themselves or their secrets. Whoever had killed him must have felt threatened. Or it had been a robbery gone bad, but for some reason, the killer hadn't had time to get the reporter's keys to go through his car. She wasn't ruling out that possibility. She hoped it was the more likely possibility, but the niggling in her gut told her she was probably wrong. She first suspected Decatur Williams, but Finche's time of death estimate didn't correlate with the time Mrs. Williams had met with him. Her alibi was solid.

Grams and Agatha excused themselves after they'd all pitched in to clean up after dinner. This gave Jake and Lexi time to catch up and cuddle on the couch in front of a toasty fire. She carried a tray of tea and cookies into the living room so they could settle in.

Lexi snuggled under Jake's arm, enjoying the quiet and peace. She wanted to discuss things with him, but just being beside him, breathing in his scent, was more needed than anything else at the moment. They had wedding plans to talk about, too. Unfortunately, it didn't appear that a wedding would be happening anytime soon. She let out a long sigh. The circumstances and not knowing about the Danforth who was buried in the local cemetery raised a lot of doubts. Was she a descendant of the guy? And why had the people of Mystic Cove all but removed his existence from the town records? She hadn't voiced her concerns to anyone. She knew she had to share them with Jake, but a big part of her was afraid to find out the truth. Afraid that Jake couldn't handle the truth if it turned out to be bad news.

Jake rubbed her arm and kissed her on top of the head. His presence was warm and cozy. It was nice to have him home. She'd missed him more than she'd ever expected to. Secretly, she hoped he wouldn't have to go on many business trips like this.

She felt him take in a deep breath, so she raised up and looked at him. "You want to know what's been going on?"

"Yeah, but I also want to sit here quietly, with you, and not think about anything else in the world. But, I know you and John have a case to solve, and if I can help out in any way, I want to."

She grabbed the reporter's laptop and handed it to Jake. "You can start with this. I haven't even tried to look at it."

"See, I knew you were ready to jump right in," he said, a wide grin on his face. "It's not like you to not be nosy and want to jump into something. Why did you wait for me?"

"I know, but I have a weird feeling about this case, and I think I'm afraid of what I'm going to discover. Besides, we just got the laptop today and I haven't had time."

Jake reached out and squeezed her hand. "It's going to be okay. Whatever we discover, we will deal with it."

"What if the secrets in this town are something we can't recover from?"

"Lexi, you know these people are strong and resilient. They'll be okay. They're a lot tougher than you give them credit for."

"It's not them I'm worried about."

"Stop worrying, at least until we find out if there's something to worry about."

Jake booted up the laptop while Lexi started digging through some of the paper files of Norman Davis. Some of the papers were really old. Some were new printouts of old documents. Most of them were about the town, dating back only about one hundred and fifty years. She grabbed the last folder of papers and flipped it open. These files dated back to the late seventeen hundreds, the time of the previous Danforth that had lived Cryptic Cove. As she scanned them, a few local surnames stuck out. The ancestors had still lived in the area.

Jake turned the computer screen towards Lexi. "This is kind of odd. He's taken a lot of pictures around town, but for some reason he has a lot of pictures of Dell Chimay. I think he was following him."

"That is odd. He's a retired postal worker. I'm guessing he'd know almost all of the families that live around here. I wonder what that has to do with anything though."

"That's a good question." Jake said as he scrolled through more images on the computer.

Lexi flipped through the last file folder some more. Inside was a paper on something called coffin torture. It was complete with images. Supposedly, people were put into a metal or wooden cage and then tortured in public, or put on display in the town square so the town's people could poke, gouge or throw things at the person locked inside.

Another paper in the same file was an order receipt from the local hardware company. She checked the list. Many of the items could be used for such a contraption as this coffin torture thing. She gasped when she read the name on the receipt.

"What's wrong? Did you find something?" Jake asked.

She showed him the pages and the receipt. "Maybe this is why the reporter was following Mr. Chimay so closely."

Jake looked at the information. Concern crossed his face. "You should have John check into this. If Chimay caught the guy following him and he has something to hide, he could be a suspect, at least in the death of the reporter." Jake looked at her, "I want you to promise you'll let John handle this. I don't want you going off on your own and confronting this guy. He could be dangerous."

She stuffed the pages back into the folder and laid it on the coffee table before picking up her cup of tea. "I know. I'll let John deal with this." She assured Jake, but her mind was already reeling with questions and gruesome images of someone being put on display and tortured in such a heinous manner. What if he had been building this for Shirley, but things got out of hand at her place when he tried to kidnap her or something. She put the cup of tea down and grabbed the folder again. The guy could be building this thing for the upcoming Halloween set at the town square. That wasn't a far-fetched idea, was it?

Jake turned sideways, his eyes laser focused and his expression serious, "I mean it Lexi. You let John deal with this guy."

"I will. That thing scares me." She said, pointing to the folder.

Jake went back to work on the computer files. She could tell he had his doubts because trouble seemed to find her, and yeah, sometimes she did go off on her own to investigate. But, she was trying to do better and not get herself into situations, with bad guys or with Jake.

Chapter 13

Lexi showed John the papers and photos that she and Jake had discovered on the reporter's laptop. There was still a lot to go through, but John agreed that he needed to speak with Mister Dell Chimay and find out what he knew. He grabbed a cup of coffee to go and told her he'd be gone an hour or so. Mr. Chimay lived on a farm just outside of town.

Lexi flipped through more of the reporter's files, but didn't find anything significant, so she decided to stare at the diner across the street. It was the first place she'd seen Jake after she'd arrived in town the year before.

She started thinking about the current case. Was it possible that Dell had killed Shirley and the reporter? What would he gain from digging into the town secrets? He was always a friendly guy, but that didn't always mean anything when it came to secrets; whether someone wanted to hide them or reveal them.

A large man entering the diner caught her attention. It was Dell Chimay. Crap, John was gone to speak to him. She dialed John's cell phone number and heard it ringing from his office. Double crap! He'd left his phone at the office, which was something he was good at because he wasn't used to carrying one. Surely he'd be back soon when he discovered that Dell wasn't at home. Of course, it'd take him twenty minutes to get to Dell's place and another twenty minutes to get back into town. A whole forty minutes, and that was if he didn't run into anyone to chat with. Another thing John was good at was chatting with people for long periods of time, sometimes losing track of time.

Dangit! She couldn't take the risk that the man would be gone by the time John returned, but she had promised Jake she wouldn't question the man and get herself into any trouble. He was in a public place, so what could it hurt to go over and try to get some information out of him?

She stood up just as her phone rang. She looked at the Caller ID. Apparently her decision was made, she couldn't ignore a phone call from the sheriff's office. She didn't want to take the call either, but that was beside the point. She sat back down and picked up the receiver.

Chapter 14

Lexi met with the ladies that afternoon at Crystal Scents. They normally met for morning coffee, but Grams had called and asked her to stop by.

When she arrived, the ladies were in a deep discussion. They turned to look at her. Mavis Clark, the town's Magistrate, who was normally a cranky old bat, was the first one to speak. "Come on in, Lexi. I think I have something you'll be interested in."

Lexi walked on in while Mavis kept talking and sifting through the papers in front of her. "As you know, a lot of the old town records have disappeared. We can't figure out why, but I did go through some old boxes that were stuffed into the corner of the basement at my office." She found the paper she was looking for while she took a breath. She held out the paper. "I found this one stuffed in a box with other old records, but the strange thing is, this paper had nothing to do with the others. Either someone shoved it in there by mistake, or maybe they wanted to hide it quickly and never got back around to it."

Lexi hesitated before taking the paper. She'd never heard Mavis speak in such an upbeat manner. Oh, she always had plenty to say, but it was usually mean, rude and dripping with sarcasm. Lexi suspected she'd been drinking. She definitely wasn't acting like her typical self.

She noticed Lexi staring at her. "Don't worry dear, I'm just excited to find this paper. I do get excited, you know. I'll be back to my old grumpy self when all this blows over."

At least the woman knew she was out of character. Lexi looked down at the paper. The name was the same as the one on the old crypt in the cemetery. William H. Danforth. Her eyes grew wide as she looked back up at Mavis who began to point out a few things.

"As you can see, he owned many of the properties here in town. The thing I find odd is that his home address is missing. It's been purposely scratched out. So we have no clue who in town now owns that property and what could be hidden on it."

"You're right. If we could figure that out and search the place, we might find some of the lost information, or at least some clue as to why the town decided to hide or destroy the old records. It could also tell us what the killer is after."

Ms. Jensen had been quiet the whole time, but she finally spoke. "What if the killer is looking for that property, too? We don't know who else could be in danger."

Agatha piped in, "What if that reporter found the property, and whoever killed Shirley also killed him so he couldn't tell anyone else. The killer may already know where that property is."

Grams eased forward to join the conversation. "I think it's time we all start trying to remember what our grandparents hid.

Ms. Jensen raised her voice, but the words squeaked out of her mouth. "For goodness sakes, Velda, that was over fifty years ago. We were just children."

"I know, but the elders told us to remember when we got older, and the Cryptex was turned over to one of us. How have we gotten so lax in all these years. Our weekly card games used to include discussions about the things hidden. Now the hidden has become the forgotten." Grams replied.

"Apparently, someone hasn't forgotten about the hidden, and they are going to great lengths to make sure this town's secrets are uncovered." Ms. Jensen said, wringing her hands as she paced the floor.

"Well, we probably shouldn't have allowed this to be buried," Mavis Clark spoke calmly, "but we never expected any of this to come back to haunt us."

Agatha stood up and looked at the other ladies, "I didn't even think it was real. I thought the elders were just paranoid and had overactive imaginations. But after what I've been through, there's people in this world who do awful things, and will go to any lengths necessary to get what they want."

The ladies shook their heads in unison.

Grams reached out and rubbed Agatha's arm, "It has come back to haunt us. We know it's real now, or at least someone believes it is. That's why it's so important for us to remember, or at least do our best to find out."

"I'm not so sure we should be digging into it now, either." Ms. Jensen said. She had been visibly shaken during the whole conversation.

As the oldest of the ladies, she was probably the most afraid of bad things happening. She lived alone, so it was understandable that she would be afraid, especially with no idea who the killer could go after next.

Lexi took the paper Mavis had found and headed back to the office. She wanted to look over the properties listed and dig through some old maps. She hoped some of the locations still existed, but it was doubtful. People buy property, tear down old buildings and replace them with new ones. Maybe she could find a pattern or at least figure out which parts of town were the oldest and which buildings might have some clues hidden somewhere inside.

She thought back to what Grams had said about the Cryptex. John had been upset when he saw it. He'd left the office with it in his pocket the afternoon of Shirley's death. It hadn't really been mentioned since then. Lexi had no clue where he'd taken it, but it was time to ask him. The item apparently came with its share of danger and bad omens. The morgue and constable's office had already been ransacked, as had the library. Whatever the killer wanted had something to do with that item. Lexi looked at the paper in her hand. Obviously, these locations could hold clues too.

Chapter 15

Friday night was a welcome relief. It had been a week since the death of Shirley and a few days since the murder of the reporter. Jake and Lexi looked forward to the dinner Peyton had planned and prepared. It was supposed to be for planning the wedding, but Lexi had a feeling they'd end up talking about everything else that was happening.

They arrived to find Charlie and Paisley on the living room floor with boxes and plastic pieces.

Paisley looked up with a huge smile on her face, "Look Aunt Lexi and Uncle Jake, Charlie got us these cool drones. We're going out tomorrow to fly them around."

Jake headed in their direction to join in on the assembly process. "That's so cool." He said as he rubbed the top of her head.

"We can even take pictures and movies with them." Paisley exclaimed, her face lit up. Lexi's heart pinched seeing her happy and smiling again after the ordeal several months back. Since that time, Charlie had taken up with her, and they were now best buds. Peyton refused to acknowledge the fact that there was something between herself and Charlie on a personal level, but it was definitely apparent that he'd stepped in as a big brother, or father figure, for Paisley, and she was fast becoming a well-rounded child again.

Lexi headed to the kitchen to help Peyton with last minute details for getting the meal on the table.

As she looked back into the living room, her heart melted at the laughter and smiles coming from the three engineers who were working hard to get their project put together. "Charlie and Paisley sure are close now." She said as she turned back towards the kitchen. "It's so good to see that she's gotten past that whole mess."

Peyton's face beamed. "Charlie has been really good for her. And he's really good to her too. I'm afraid he may spoil her rotten." She paused, "I just hope she doesn't get hurt if he finds a girlfriend and doesn't have time for her."

Lexi let out a snort, trying to hold back a laugh. "What? I don't think that's funny."

"I'm laughing at you. In case you haven't noticed, Charlie only has eyes for you, sweetie. He's not going to go off looking for a girlfriend unless you completely reject him. And I have a sneaking suspicion that's not going to happen, because you have feelings for him, too."

"Don't be silly." Peyton turned away.

"I'm not. Everyone else in town sees it. I don't know why you can't admit it."

Peyton shook her head and let out a sigh. "I guess I'm not ready. We both know how my last relationship turned out, so let's get you married off before we start worrying about my life."

"Fair enough, but you know this whole situation with Charlie is different. You know he truly loves you and Paisley."

Peyton grabbed bowls of food, turning away to hide the grin that spread across her face. Lexi didn't say any more. Instead she left Peyton with the thought of a super great guy being in love with her. It was a good place to end the conversation.

After dinner, they all gathered in the living room. Paisley was excited to finish putting together the new drone. Lexi served coffee and pastries for dessert. It was nice having a quiet evening with friends, but the group also had a knack for turning their conversations towards whatever was going on in town that was hot on the gossip train. Tonight was no different. Peyton asked if Lexi and John made any progress in the case. She didn't want to talk about the murders in front of Paisley, so she mentioned the paper and the properties listed on it. No harm in discussing an intriguing mystery of town history. But it also meant that she had to face the fact that this town didn't want any remembrance of the person whose surname she carried. She didn't have a clue if they were related or not, but she was also starting to lose her belief in coincidences. The niggling feeling in her gut told her she was kin to this person. It wasn't a good feeling either. Why else would the town try to destroy any evidence that the man had ever existed?

Chapter 16

Saturday morning at the office had been pretty quiet. It was a nice change of pace. Lexi looked over the paper Mavis Clark had given her with some property listings, along with a few other papers she had found. Nothing was coming together. Most of the properties listed on the paper had been torn down and replaced with new buildings over a hundred years ago, so there wasn't much to go on, and no chance of them having a basement where old documents could be kept. Or was there? Would they have filled in the holes in the ground and destroyed the basements too, or just built on top of them? She decided she'd walk around town later in the afternoon to look at some things. The town was always quiet during the weekend, so it was the perfect time to just wander around and not have to worry about running into all the busy-bodies that were out during the week.

She laid the paper aside and rubbed her temples, the case was taking its toll on her brain.

Movement caught her attention, and she looked up just in time to see Charlie, Peyton and Paisley walk up to the glass door and wave at her. She could definitely use the break.

Paisley bounced into the office. She was as excited as she was the night before when putting her new drone together. "Aunt Lexi! Aunt Lexi! You'll never guess what me and Charlie did this morning."

Lexi play-pinched her nose. "You went out to play with your new toys."

"We did, but that's not the coolest part!"

"What's the coolest part?"

"We found something. It's so awesome." She turned to look at Charlie. "Show her Charlie. Show her what we found."

Charlie pulled a USB flash drive out of his pocket. "Can I borrow your computer for a minute?"

"Sure," Lexi said as she got up and let him have control of the machine. For someone who was raised without any electronic devices, he'd picked up on computers and other stuff super quick. It was like he had a computer brain himself. She was still amazed at how smart the guy was and how fast knowledge went into his brain.

He looked up at Lexi. "We went up to the area around Hayden's Ridge. We wanted to get some video and pictures of the cliffs overlooking the ocean. Those are areas we never get to see up close."

"True," Lexi replied. "Unless you want to be a rock climber."

Charlie laughed. "Not me. I prefer to stay as close to the ground as possible."

"We found some eagle's nests, Aunt Lexi." Paisley piped in.

Lexi turned to look at her. "Wow! That's really cool."

"Yeah, but you don't want to make them mad so we didn't get real close. Charlie was afraid they'd attack our drones and destroy them."

"I bet they would."

"But that's not the best thing we found," Charlie said.

Lexi turned back to him. He motioned for her to come around behind the desk so she could see the computer screen. "I've got the video loaded now.

This is close to the cliffs. We were flying over the wooded area, behind the bungalows up there on the ridge. I couldn't tell much on the iPad mini when I was flying over, but after we got home and uploaded the videos to the computer and looked with a bigger screen—well, it got quite interesting."

"Really?" She asked, staring at the computer screen. There were a lot of trees and a few open spaces. One spot caught her eye. She bent over to get a closer look when Charlie paused the video. "Is that what I think it is?"

"I believe so. Amazing isn't it?"

"Definitely."

"Now that I know it's there, we're going to go back, but we wanted you to see this first. I'll take the drone in low and check it out a lot better. I may even take Peyton's laptop. It has a bigger screen than the little iPad, so I should be able to see more on the screen."

"That's a good idea. I can't believe this. Why has no one ever told us that was there?"

Charlie pointed at the screen again. "Well right here, you can definitely see there's a house, a big house. And if you look down this way a little bit, you can see the remains of some kind of garden. There's a definite pattern there."

"Oh my gosh!"

Charlie and Peyton both looked at her. "What?" They asked in unison.

"I've seen that pattern before." She said as she opened the file folder that was lying on the desk and pulled out a picture. "It's small, but that's the same symbol that's on the old Danforth mausoleum at the cemetery." She walked over to the chair by the windows and sat down.

Peyton sat down beside her. "You think that estate belonged to him?"

"It has to, but that's not the only place I've seen that symbol."

"Where else have you seen it?"

Lexi sat in silence for a moment. she hadn't told them much about the object Shirley had been clutching when she died. She didn't know how much she should tell them. People were getting killed, and it obviously had something to do with that symbol, but she decided they needed to know. Their safety was important, so the more they knew, the more alert they could be to look for strange happenings or people.

"The item Shirley had in her hand when she died. It has that symbol on it."

"Wow!" Charlie said. "I think I definitely need to go back up there and get some more video."

"Wait!" Lexi said as she stood up. "That may not be a great idea. Someone is after that Cryptex thing, and this symbol seems to tie a lot of things together. It could be dangerous."

Charlie walked over and rubbed her arm. "I think you know I can take care of myself."

She looked up at him. Okay, so he *is* some kind of kung fu expert, but she was still worried. "Okay, but don't take Paisley with you. She doesn't need to be there if anything goes wrong. Actually, I'd feel a lot better if you got Jake to go with you. And don't tell anyone."

Charlie snapped his fingers, "That's a great cover story too. I can't wait to show Jake my new drone. Of course, we have to go out and let him play with it." He winked at Lexi. It eased her fears some, but not a lot.

So much for a quiet day. Her nerves were now more on edge than they had ever been. She still couldn't figure out what the relation was, but that symbol was not a coincidence. Was it possible the killer was looking for that location? Was there something in that estate that was worth killing over? She knew there must be something really bad up there. Why else would the whole town try to wipe it out of existence?

Chapter 17

Lexi went by Crystal Scents to find out the latest news from the ladies on her way home . Her Grams and Ms. Jensen were busy making their candles. The aroma filled her nostrils. She took in a deep breath and let the vanilla and sugar cookie scent fill her nose. It brought back memories of her childhood. Grams' kitchen always smelled so good, but her fondest memories were of her making sugar cookies into shapes. She had animal shapes, cars, houses and people too. They always had a great time decorating them.

"We're in the back." Grams called out, so she headed to the back of the store. They were just pouring up the last few jars of the wonderful scented wax. In each jar was a precious gemstone, but once the wax hardened you had to burn the candle to see which gemstone treasure was in the bottom.

"They smell wonderful, Grams. They remind me of baking cookies with you when I was a little girl," Lexi said as she walked over to the table. The white wax was still transparent enough that she could see the colorful gemstones they'd placed into the bottom of each one. Thoughts of the Cryptex entered her mind. It had something hidden inside it. That she was sure of. Unfortunately, no one alive knew what that was. And no clue how to even open the thing to find out what treasure, or curse, it held. She didn't even know where it was. John had left the office with it days before, but wouldn't tell her what he had done with it.

Charlie had discovered an old estate with the same pattern in the garden hedges. He and Jake would be going back to the area and flying a drone overhead. They all talked about going out there and walking the woods until they found the place, but the guys insisted they should investigate it from the air before anyone tried to make their way through all the underbrush. They swore each other to secrecy until they learned more. Whoever was after the Cryptex could also be looking for that old estate. Somehow it was tied to the Danforth family name, but Lexi wasn't any closer to finding answers about that either.

As soon as she, Grams and Ms. Jensen had cleaned up their work area, she pulled out a picture she had taken at the mausoleum to show them the symbol. It was a long shot, but she hoped they could remember something from when they were children. Surely they had been to the cemetery and saw it, or perhaps the woods up at Hayden's Ridge hadn't been so thick back then, and they knew the old estate was there.

"I wanted to ask about this symbol that keeps showing up in our investigation. Can you tell me anything about it?"

Grams looked at the picture, but quickly turned away and started cleaning the counter she'd already wiped down. Ms. Jensen looked at the picture and practically did the same thing.

"You two know something and you need to tell me. I need to know why this symbol scares everyone, and more importantly, why it's attached to my last name."

Grams stopped what she was doing and looked at her. "Some things are better off buried." She pointed to the picture. "That's one of them."

"But Grams, Shirley was killed because of this. We need to know why. Someone wants whatever is in that Cryptex and it all relates to this symbol. They may even kill again to get their hands on it. Keeping things buried is why all this is happening."

The two women looked at each other. Grams put down the towel she was using to wipe the counters. "You're right. We will do what we can to remember."

Lexi left Crystal Scents with the intention of going to the library. Surely there were some old records left that had some information. She would need to keep it quiet . She couldn't very well go in there and tell Mrs. Williams what she was looking for. The woman already didn't like her and would think she was nuts. Mrs. Williams had gotten pretty protective over the old town files that were in the library.

On the way, she decided to stop and talk to Mavis Clark, the town Magistrate, instead. Something gave her a feeling she'd know more about this than the library. She was in charge of town records, and she was also very interested in real estate in the area. It's possible she knew more than she let on. Lexi turned right at the corner to head to her office, instead of taking a left to go to the library.

Mavis and Lexi had never really gotten along. In fact, no one in town got along with Mavis very well. She liked to stir things up. She and Grams had had their share of rifts over the years. The biggest one was right after Lexi moved back home and a murder had occurred. Mavis liked to gouge old wounds. After that though, they came to a truce. They'd even become friends, in an odd way. Perhaps they decided it was time for the older locals to start sticking together.

When Lexi walked in the door, Mavis Clark looked up at her and smiled. A chill ran through Lexi's body. Her smiles were always more cause for alarm than her snarls. Lexi reminded herself that was in the past. The woman was a lot nicer now. She pulled the picture out with reluctance, unsure if she wanted to share it with anyone else, plus it always bothered her when Ms. Clark was in a pleasant mood.

In fact, she would have preferred her to be in a bad mood. It was easier to tell if she was hiding something.

"I hate to bother you," Lexi said, as she walked up to her desk.

"Nonsense. You enjoy bothering people." A smirk crossed her face. "But that's why I like you. You remind me of me."

"Oh? I'm not sure if that's a compliment or not."

Mavis let out a hearty laugh. "I'm not either. What's that in your hand?" She asked, pointing to the picture.

Lexi sucked in a deep breath, not really sure how to even ask about the matter, but she handed it over to her. "This symbol keeps showing up in our investigation."

Mavis looked at the picture. Her brows pinched together.

"Since you have an interest in real estate, I wondered if you'd seen it before."

She handed the picture back. "There's a lot of people who think the past should stay hidden and buried."

"Are you one of them?"

Mavis grabbed the mug off her desk before getting up and going to the coffee maker. She poured herself a cup, turned around and leaned against the counter. "I was," she said before taking a sip from the cup. "But now, I'm not so sure it's best to sweep things under the rug, especially the old secrets our grandparents wanted to hide."

She returned to her chair.

"Do you know what those secrets are?"

"Only bits I remember from childhood. Shirley was always aware, and now she's dead because of it."

"How do you know her death is related."

"Because she told me."

"Excuse me?" Lexi's mouth dropped open. "How could she tell you? She's dead."

Mavis frowned. "She gave me a warning, before she was murdered. I didn't think much about it at the time, so I pretty much blew it off."

Lexi reached into her bag and grabbed a picture of the Cryptex. "Have you ever seen this?"

Mavis glanced at the picture, a look of fear shot through her eyes. She took the picture and stared at it for a long time. "I haven't seen this since I was a little girl. Where did you get it?"

"I can't say. We're looking into a lot of things."

"Shirley had it, didn't she?" Her voice trailed off, a faraway look on her face as she spoke the words.

The door opened and Lexi turned to see the retired postmaster, Dell Chimay, walk in.

Mavis quickly handed the picture back, almost shoving it into Lexi's hands. "I'm sorry, I can't help you."

"No problem." Lexi stammered the words out. "I need to get back to the office. Thank you for your time."

She turned towards Mr. Chimay and extended her hand, "I don't think we've ever been properly introduced. I'm Velda's granddaughter, Lexi."

"Yes," he said, as he held up a bandaged hand. "Pardon me if I don't shake."

"Oh my, what happened?"

"I had an accident. It'll be fine." He glanced around at Mavis. Lexi could tell he was anxious to speak with her, so she said her goodbyes. It was no secret that he and Mavis had some kind of real estate competition going on so she didn't mind leaving. She wasn't in the mood to listen to them argue over a piece of property. According to Grams, their discussions could get pretty heated.

Chapter 18

As she left the Magistrate's office her phone rang. It was Decatur Williams, from the library. *Odd timing*, she thought to herself. Apparently the librarian had been going through more old files and ran across some Lexi might find interesting. She had planned to stop by the library, so this was just the excuse she needed. On the way, she decided she'd just get the papers from Mrs. Williams and not push her luck asking to see any more files.

Back at the office, she grabbed a cup of coffee and started rummaging through the old town records that Mrs. Williams had given her. Most of them were practically useless. Lexi wondered why she thought they could be of help, but she found one page that was stuck between two other pages. It was literally stuck, causing her to almost miss it. She gently pulled one of the pages away from it. The ink had faded, and some of the words from the other pages had transposed themselves onto the page she wanted to read, but she could make out the distinct drawing on the page. The symbol from the Cryptex and the old mausoleum. She squinted to make out the words written beneath it, but only the name Danforth was legible enough.

Her eyes grew tired and strained, and some of the words looked to be in Latin or some strange language. She packed the pages into her bag and decided she'd stop to see Peyton on the way home. A fresh pair of eyes would be good.

Peyton never ceased to amaze her. She took the page and scanned it into her computer, increased the contrast and some other stuff, then printed out the result. A lot of the text was still garbled, but they could make out more of the words. The page was also full of symbols, which they didn't understand. They looked like some of those Egyptian hieroglyphics.

Jake called to find out if Lexi had left the office for the day. She explained she was at the B&B with Peyton. He and Charlie were headed back to town, so it was the perfect opportunity for them to all meet up again. The girls started preparing some sandwiches so they could eat while sharing all the discoveries they'd found.

"How did it go?" Lexi asked as Jake kissed her on the cheek.

"Kinda strange, to be honest. Baxter was there." He pulled something out of his pocket. "He actually helped guide the drone around to some interesting places. He even flew into a broken window of the house."

"Really. Do you have footage of the inside?"

"No, we were afraid we'd lose the signal, but he came out with this and dropped it into my hand." Jake said as he handed Lexi an old coin. "It has the same symbol and some others we haven't seen before."

She looked the coin over. "Oh my gosh. Mrs. Williams gave me a box of some old records today she had found in the backroom of the library. One of the pages has these same markings. Peyton enhanced it so we could have a printout." She grabbed one of the printed sheets and handed it to Jake.

Charlie picked up one of the copies and looked it over. "If I'm not mistaken, these are Runes."

"What?" Everyone asked in unison.

"Runes. They're an alphabet. It's been a long time since I've read up on that stuff, but now they're used for divination, like tarot cards and other stuff."

Peyton looked at the coin and the symbols on the page they'd printed out. "I don't know if I like where this is going. Maybe our grandparents hid all of this stuff for a very good reason."

Lexi looked at her. "I agree, but we have to get to the bottom of this. Whoever is after the Cryptex and the secrets from the past are willing to kill for it. If we can expose the secrets and get it all out in the open, it will put a stop to all this nonsense."

"You're right," Peyton replied. "Let's grab the sandwiches and then watch the video the guys made. Maybe we can figure out more of this puzzle."

Charlie loaded the files onto the computer and everyone settled in. The place was overgrown, but there was quite a bit of open space too. Just like Jake said, Baxter swooped in and guided the drone through the trees and other areas. It was like he knew what the guys were trying to get a better look at. Smart bird.

At the end of the video, when the drone was flying back to the road so the guys could land it, a car on the side of the road was clearly visible. "I've seen that car." Lexi said.

"Where?" Jake asked.

"It was recent. Oh wait! It was today. I went to see Mavis Clark and old man Chimay showed up. When I walked outside, that car was parked in front. It must belong to Dell Chimay."

"Could that be a coincidence?" Peyton asked.

Lexi shrugged her shoulders. "I don't know, but he also has a bandage on his hand. What if it's a burn and he's the one who started the fire at Shirley's?"

Jake looked at Lexi. "You're jumping to conclusions."

"I am, but isn't it strange that he not only showed up when I was trying to talk to Mavis, but before that he'd been in the same woods as you guys. And, it's very close to that old estate?"

Peyton's eyes grew wide. "He and Shirley had a thing going on not too long ago, too."

Everyone looked at her. "What kind of thing?" Lexi asked.

"You know, a relationship thing. They were seeing each other."

Lexi turned to Jake. "Still think I'm jumping to conclusions?"

"Yeah, but that's a lot of coincidences, and I don't believe in coincidences."

"I need to let John know about all of this. We can talk to Mr. Chimay tomorrow. John tried today, but he missed him."

Lexi gathered up all the pages and put them into a file folder. Charlie made her a copy of the video and saved it to a flash drive. For the first time since Shirley's death, Lexi felt like they finally had a lead. She didn't want to wait until morning to speak to John, so she called and asked him to meet her at Grams' to show him all of the new evidence.

Chapter 19

John and Lexi got an early start the following morning. He didn't have the suspicions Lexi did, but he agreed with her that it was all too coincidental. Shirley and Dell did have a relationship recently. Grams had confirmed that it ended with some anger on both sides. Grams didn't know if they'd ever discussed town secrets, or if the man even knew about the object Shirley had kept hidden all these years, but everyone agreed that if they were getting close, knowing Dell's family were original town members, it could have come up.

"Perhaps he got greedy or something." Grams said. "Thinking a hidden treasure exists can make people do awful things."

"I know he lives a modest life, but wouldn't his retirement from the postal service be a pretty good income?" Lexi asked.

John reminded the ladies how greed can affect people. They'd seen it right after Lexi moved back to

Cryptic Cove and the manager at Hayden's Ridge had been stealing people's money.

John turned his truck down the long driveway. Dell Chimay was coming out of his workshop. He turned quickly and shut the large door. It looked suspicious to Lexi, but she didn't say anything to John. Hopefully he caught it, too.

The questioning took a turn for the worst when the old man took offence at Lexi's accusation. "You saw the bandage on my hand in Mavis Clark's office and automatically assume I killed Shirley? You've got a lot of nerve, young lady. And your investigative reasoning is so far-fetched it's not even funny. It don't even deserve a response."

John spoke up, "Now Dell, you have to admit your actions are a bit suspicious, like you're trying to hide something. What's in your workshop that you don't want to talk about or you don't want us to see?"

Dell shook his head. "It's a special project, it's a surprise. I'd appreciate it if you'd just drop it."

"I can't do that. You know it. I'm the town constable, and it's my responsibility to check every lead. I came out here today giving you the benefit of the doubt, but after your attitude and your sneaky behavior, I have to wonder what's going on." John said.

"Do you have one of them confidential clauses like lawyer's do?"

"What do you mean?"

"I mean, if I show you what's in my shop, will it stay a secret? Between us?"

"That depends on what you're hiding and if it's legal."

"I ain't hiding nothing, John. It's just a special project, and I need it to stay a secret until I'm ready. I ain't doing nothing illegal."

"You'll have to let me be the judge of that. If it's not illegal, and it has nothing to do with our case, then I promise you, we'll keep your secret."

"What about her?" Dell barked out as he pointed to Lexi.

"She will keep your secret."

"Okay then, but if word of this gets out, I'll tell the whole town you railroaded me."

"That sounds like a threat."

"Only because this is important to me."

"Okay, just show me what's so super secretive."

Dell led John and Lexi into his shop. Along each wall was a wooden scene he'd cut out and painted. The work was beautiful. Lexi's mouth gaped open as she looked at him, "It's a Nativity scene."

"Of course it's a Nativity scene. I told you I wasn't no killer. We've been using the same scene at the courthouse for decades and I thought it was time to build a new one. I want to present it to the town at Thanksgiving, before we start putting out all the Christmas stuff."

John looked at Dell. "I'm sorry we doubted you. This is a wonderful gesture and a beautiful gift for the town."

Dell shuffled some dirt with the tip of his boot before looking back up at John. "I didn't mean to be so rude about it. I know you have a job to do. We're all in shock about Shirley, and we all miss her."

"You and her had been seeing each other. So, you can see why we'd need to question you."

"Yeah, but you could've come out here in a nicer way instead of just jumping to conclusions and making accusations."

"And you could've been less defensive and suspicious acting."

"Agreed." Dell said as he reached out to shake John's hand. "I hope you figure this out. It's had me all upset. I've just poured myself into this project so I don't sit around and think about it."

"I understand." John told him.

They left the Chimay farm with no more answers than they had before. Either the man was telling the truth, or he was using it all as a good coverup. Lexi told John she would check with the hospital to see when Dell was treated, if he was treated. Learning of his town project hadn't completely marked him off the suspect list, but it did move him down a notch or two.

Chapter 20

John dropped Lexi off at her vehicle, and she headed to the hardware store to check on Dell Chimay's purchases. The man had a good alibi, there was no doubt about that, but they still had to follow up on his story.

Melvin Goode was a cheerful man, always had a kind word for everyone. For his age, he was in great shape and very spry. The years showed on his face, but it was a sweet face. Lexi thought of her grandfather whenever she ran into Melvin. They both had smiles that would light up a room, compassionate eyes and always a warm glow about them. At least that's what she remembered of her grandfather, and that definitely described Melvin.

As soon as he spotted her, he came around the counter, his arms spread wide. "My dear Miss Lexi. Give this old man a hug. How are you?"

"I'm good. At least I think I'm good. There's so much going on right now that it's hard to catch my breath."

He released her from his embrace and looked into her eyes. "Oh yes, the wedding plans. How is that coming along?"

Emotions welled up inside Lexi. "As much as I'm ready to enjoy our big day, the plans have kinda reached a stand-still. This new investigation is so overwhelming and emotional."

He reached out and rubbed her arm. "Don't forget to focus on the good things in life, too. The wedding will happen when it's the right time."

"I know. It's just so hard right now. And we need to figure out who killed Shirley, so we can get back to normal and focus on the good stuff."

"I understand. What can I help you with?"

"I hate to ask, but it is an investigation and we have to check every possible lead. We've talked to Dell Chimay, and he's been working on a secret project. Can you tell me about the purchases he's made lately?"

"Yes, I keep all sales records. Since he has an account with us, all of his purchases are logged into his account."

"That's great."

"Are you looking for anything specific?"

She couldn't tell him they suspected the man could have burned Shirley, or maybe even started fires at the cemetery, but she needed to know if he'd bought stuff to start a fire with. "Well, I can't really discuss details, but I also need to know if anyone has purchased flammable materials lately. There was some vandalism at the cemetery. It's probably not related, but since I'm here, I might as well find out what I can on that case, too."

"There was a kid in here about a week ago. He was asking about liquids that could be burned. I couldn't sell to him, of course, because of his age. He said it was for a school project, but it did strike me as odd."

"Who was it?"

"I didn't recognize him. He talked like he's from around here, but I'd never seen him before."

Lexi looked around. "I don't suppose you have security cameras?"

"There's a few, but they only cover certain areas of the store. I can give you what footage I have. Maybe he crossed in front of one of them."

"That'd be great."

Lexi left the hardware store with a stack of purchase invoices, a few descriptions of people that had bought specific items and no more answers than she had before. Melvin gave her a good description of the kid, so if he was on any of the surveillance footage, he'd be easy to spot. The more she thought about it, the more she decided they needed to find out who this kid was. If he was responsible for the fires and destruction at the cemetery, he could very well be responsible for Shirley's death. Maybe he'd been trying to rob her, and everything else was a mere coincidence.

Lexi shared her thoughts with John. He agreed that the kid could be a likely suspect.

"Do you think all of this could be about a robbery and not even about that Cryptex or town secrets."

"That would be a relief." John said, "But we can't let our guard down where that thing is concerned. It may not be linked to anything. Unfortunately, it has come to the surface, and we need to solve that mystery, even if it's not related to the vandalism or Shirley's death.

Lexi spent the afternoon going through the security video footage that Melvin had turned over to her.

Chapter 21

Peyton and Lexi got together after work to look over the enhanced pages. Peyton had taken it on herself to study up on runes to find out what they meant and how they could relate to the case.

Peyton poured two cups of tea. "I've been looking over that paper," she said as she set the two cups down on the table. "It seems that one of those symbols, the one shaped like an R, is called Raidho, and it means the journey is the destination." She pointed to the other one, "This one that looks like a C means the student surpasses the teacher. It's called Kenaz."

Lexi took a sip of the tea. "It's awfully cryptic, isn't it."

"It is, but I'm guessing that someone who has more knowledge of these things probably understands the deeper meanings."

"What about this other shape?" Lexi asked, pointing to the diagram. "I've seen it before, on TV shows and stuff."

"It's called a triquetra. In some cultures, it symbolizes a triple goddess or something, but it could also indicate the holy trinity."

"I have a gut feeling that my ancestor used it more for this goddess thing. If he was a good guy, why would the whole town try to hide and bury everything related to him?" Lexi said as she set the cup of tea on the table.

"That's what I've been wondering. Don't worry though, we'll find out."

Lexi stood up and walked over to the patio doors. "I'm not real sure I want to find out. Maybe he wasn't a very nice man."

"I can understand your reluctance. I don't think I'd want to know either."

"But, on the other hand, people have been killed over whatever secrets are hidden behind those symbols. The sooner we do find out, the sooner we can solve this case and it can't hurt us anymore. That doesn't stop my fear though." She looked out the window. "Who's that kid out there with Charlie?" She asked, looking down into Peyton's garden.

Peyton walked over and stood beside Lexi. "Oh, that's Bobby. He lives up at the old mining community."

"What's that? Where is that? I've never heard of it."

"Some of our grandparents worked in a mine. When it collapsed and they couldn't work it anymore, several people decided to stay there instead of moving back to town. They've built this community up there, but it's more like a ghost town. I think most of the people still live in one room shacks like they did all those years ago."

"Really? It sounds awful."

"I think it is. But Charlie goes up there and talks to the people. They don't really like outsiders, but since he wasn't actually raised in town either, they trust him."

Lexi watched Charlie and the kid pull dead flowers and weeds out of the garden. Something about his appearance bothered her, but she couldn't put her finger on it. "The kid seems to like flowers."

"Yes, he's very good with them. I'm glad Charlie is helping him get used to people and being in town."

"How long has he been coming into town?"

"A few months, I guess. He helps keep the flowers pruned back. He even likes to take the ones that are still good with him when he leaves."

"That's it!" Lexi gasped.

"That's what?"

"The fresh flowers at the cemetery. They're from your garden. He's the one putting them there."

"You think so?"

"I can't be sure, but all the plastic flowers had been removed from the graves and burned. Some of the residents called after the vandalism story hit the news and reported that plastic flowers were missing from their loved ones headstones, but that fresh flowers were in their place." Lexi took in a deep breath. "And this kid may be our little pyro. I have to talk to him."

Peyton grabbed her arm. "You can't do that."

Lexi glared at Peyton, trying to figure out why she was keeping her from talking to the boy. "Why not?"

"Because, he's still afraid of people. You could scare him off and he'd never want to come back into town."

"But I have to find out if he's the one that set those fires and vandalized the mausoleum."

"We will find out, but we'll have Charlie question him."

Lexi looked back at the kid again. "Are you sure? It goes against what I've learned about investigating, and we need those answers soon."

"Trust me, I know a lot about dealing with kids. I will have Charlie talk to him when he takes him back to the mining camp later this evening."

Lexi smiled, "You definitely know how to handle kids better than I do, so I'm going to trust your gut on this one. I need to let John know, though." Lexi said as she pulled out her cellphone and punched in John's speed dial code.

After the phone call she zoomed her camera phone in on the kid and snapped a picture. It didn't hurt to have a visual so she could show John the following morning. Maybe he even knew the kid since he'd been here all his life.

For such a tiny town, it sure did seem to have a lot of secrets and things people had forgotten about. That was understandable, all communities forget their past history. But Cryptic Cove had gone to great lengths to not only forget, but to hide it as well. She had to keep digging, even though her gut told her she wouldn't like what she'd discover about the Danforth man. If he was evil, could that same evil be in her blood? Chills ran through her body at the thought. She tried to push it out of her mind. She didn't want to think about it, and figured she was jumping to conclusions and making too many speculations. It was best to focus on Shirley's death and find out what this kid knew about it and the fires. Her heart sank as she thought about where this case could be going. Surely someone that young couldn't burn a woman to rob her, but Lexi knew all too well that bad things were sometimes done by young kids. If he was guilty, the news could shake this town to it's very core. In a lot of ways it was like a fairytale town. The majority of people were kind and loving, the children were pleasant. Even the bratty kids had a sense of caring for others. If a young kid like this could do something so heinous and purposefully, what kind of message would that send to the other kids?

Chapter 22

Lexi got home a little late that evening and headed straight for her room. Flopping on her bed was a welcome relief. It had been a long, hard day and she needed a few minutes to unwind. She leaned back against the headboard and stared at herself in the mirror across the room. She looked tired. The thought occurred that she even looked old.

She glanced at her mom's tarot cards. She kept them on the dresser as a reminder. She'd never spent much time with them or even put much stock into them. Grams had said they were like a tool, a bit like affirmations or getting a sign.

She stood up, walked over to the dresser and grabbed the deck. Sitting back on the bed, she pulled them out of the box and kinda shuffled through them, mostly thinking about her mom and how much she missed her, but also about everything that was going on. The stuff Peyton and she were discovering wasn't much, but it left her feeling like something wasn't right.

She took a deep breath and pulled one of the cards out of the deck. "Okay card, tell me what I'm missing. I sure can't figure it out."

She plopped the card down on the bed. A guy carrying some swords. "Well that doesn't seem to fit the situation, does it? Unless someone is robbing the local knife shop." She giggled at how silly it sounded. She dug into the drawer of the nightstand and pulled out the book on tarot cards that Grams had given her and quickly flipped to the Seven of Swords page and started reading. Her mouth fell open. The card did fit. This card represented deception, betrayal and secret plans. It didn't give her any more to go on, but that was definitely what the town seemed to be up against.

It was crazy and left her with even more questions, so she packed the cards back into the box and returned them to the dresser. The closet door was slightly ajar so she walked over to it. *Maybe Grams had put some of her laundry away and didn't close it all the way.* She peeked inside to check. Her eyes were drawn to her mom's old hat box. The one she had discovered right after the death of her parents. She hadn't pulled it out in a long time. Everything had gotten so busy in her life that she didn't feel the need to look back at the past. But now, maybe it was time. She pulled it out and settled down on the bed with it.

As she dug through the various papers, at the bottom of the box was an old file folder. Odd, it looked similar to the ones she'd gotten from the library. She pulled it out and opened it. Her heart skipped a few beats. It was a file from Cryptic Cove. *Why did my mother have it? How did she even get it?* She read through the file. *Was this why my father moved us out of Cryptic Cove?* She headed downstairs to talk to Grams. It was time Grams finally came clean and told her the truth.

Chapter 23

Grams decided to hold a special meeting at her home. She invited the locals she'd grown up with whose families had been in the town since its inception. She also insisted that Lexi, Jake, Peyton and Charlie be there as well. With Lexi finding one of the town's files in her mom's old hat box, she felt it was necessary that everyone pooled their resources and knowledge.

Grams' living room was full of familiar faces, Mavis Clark, Ms. Jensen, the Hill family, Mrs. Drake and a few others that kept to themselves on the outskirts of town that Lexi didn't know all that well. She only knew of them from town events and the gossip train that rang her up every morning.

The town's people had more or less formed little groups, several of them whispering about what the meeting was about and why the constable wasn't out looking for Shirley's killer. Grams finally stopped fussing over getting everyone served refreshments and called the meeting to order.

"I know you're all wondering why I've called this meeting, and maybe it seems pointless when we should be looking for Shirley's killer. But, I believe we need to pool our knowledge and work together. All of us here," she said as she looked around the room, "have lived here all of our lives. Our ancestors started this town around the time of the Salem witch trials. As children, we made up stories and whispered about secrecy. I'm sure your parents, like mine, reminded you that we didn't talk about such things. The past was best left buried."

Everyone agreed and a few voiced that they'd been told the same thing by their parents or grandparents.

Grams continued, "Well, the time has come that we remember all those old stories. Even the ones we thought were just fairy tales or bedtime stories. We need to find out what this town is hiding that is worth killing over. Buried secrets have a way of coming back to haunt us. I'm sure our parents and grandparents thought it was best, but someone has remembered something, or dug something up, and they are now trying to destroy our small community. Shirley paid a dear price for what she concealed. We can't let her death be in vain."

Jasper Hill spoke up, "What are you talking about? What was Shirley hiding?"

Grams reached in her pocket and pulled out a picture to pass around. "She had this in her hand when she died. I vaguely remember seeing pictures of it as a child, or maybe I saw the real thing and don't remember. But, this is the object that is causing all the trouble. We need to find out what it is and why it's worth dying for."

"As the oldest here, Velda, I can tell you I haven't thought of those old stories since I was a child. How can you expect us to remember?" Gertie Hill asked.

Jasper Hill turned to Gertie, "Mother, I remember you telling me stories as a child. I know it's been a long time, but maybe you can remember something."

"You know my memory isn't what it used to be. That's why I moved up to Hayden's Ridge."

"I know, Mother, but in a lot of ways, you're still sharp as a tack. Maybe if you can remember some little something, it'll spark some memories for the rest of us."

Lexi looked at Gertie and Jasper. "That's an excellent idea. They teach that in psychology classes. It's similar to word association. Maybe it would help if you all focused on some event from your childhood, something you experienced together. A county fair or something like that."

"For goodness sakes, that was over fifty years ago. We were just children." Mrs. Drake rebuked.

"I know, but the elders told us to remember when we got older. How have we gotten so lax in all these years. Our weekly card game used to include discussions about the things hidden. Now the hidden has become the forgotten." Grams looked at each one of them.

"Apparently someone hasn't forgotten about the hidden, and they are going to great lengths to make sure this town's secrets are uncovered." Agatha added.

"Well, we probably shouldn't have buried them, but we never expected any of this to come back to haunt us." Grams said as she looked at her sister.

"I didn't even think it was real. I thought the elders were just paranoid and had overactive imaginations." Gertie said after a short silence. "I realize I'm the grandparent here, but my parents were hiding things too."

"It has come back to haunt us. We know it's real now, or at least someone believes it is. That's why it's so important for us to remember." Ms. Jensen said as she reached into her bag. "I didn't want anyone to know, but I have some of the missing files from the library. I'd started removing them, little by little, when I knew it was getting close to my retirement. Shirley had said something to me back then, so I thought it was best if they were kept in a more secure place, considering we didn't know who would take my place as librarian."

Mavis Clark pinched her eyebrows together. "Since Decatur Williams took over and made changes on her own without consulting anyone, it's just a mess. She's completely destroyed the system Ms. Jensen had in place."

Everyone glanced over at Ms. Jensen. She fidgeted with her fingers in her lap and then opened her mouth to speak. "I agree her methods are unconventional, but don't we have to be willing to roll with the times and accept some new ways?"

"There's nothing wrong with the old ways," spouted Mavis Clark. "I am a firm believer in 'if it ain't broke don't fix it' and there was nothing broken in the old system. Just because the whole country is going to this digital madness mess doesn't mean we have to." She crossed her arms over her chest, staring a hole into Ms. Jensen. "And you of all people are defending it. You believe in the printed word as much as I do, so what's up with you rolling with the times?"

Ms. Jensen leaned forward. "I'm just trying to help find a solution we can all live with. Things are going to change, whether we like it or not. If we can control the changes and the amount of changes, I think it's a better way to do things. Let her go digital, but let's put the old paper copies in a storage facility."

Mavis crossed her arms over her chest and leaned back. "Okay, you may have a good point."

"Ladies, we need to stay on track." Grams said, looking from Mavis to Ms. Jensen.

Lexi glanced around the room. "Why isn't Mrs. Williams here? She's the librarian now. She's been so defensive about town history when I've asked. I thought for sure she'd want in on this."

Everyone turned to look at Lexi, disbelief was on most of their faces.

Mavis Clark was the first one to speak. "She didn't grow up here. She's not one of the original families who started the town."

"Oh," Lexi said. "I assumed she was since everyone knows her and she tends to be involved in everything that goes on."

Grams let out a sigh, "She married one of the originals, but he passed away several years ago. We don't know much about her past. She's always been interested in our little town, but since she didn't grow up here, we didn't think it was relevant to invite her."

Chapter 24

After Lexi fielded all the morning gossip callers, she got a message from Peyton that Charlie was bringing Bobby by the office. She let John know before she put a hot chocolate pod in the coffee machine and got some pastries out. She wanted him to feel comfortable and food usually did the trick.

Bobby was quiet and a little timid, but well mannered.

John told him he was doing an investigation and explained that he had to ask some questions.

"Charlie explained it to me. I know I'm not in trouble if I didn't do anything wrong, and I don't think I did anything wrong."

John leaned forward in the chair. "There's been some small fires at the cemetery, some plastic flowers have been burned. Do you know who did that?"

"I did. They were old and didn't look very pretty. I didn't see a trash can close by so I went to the edge of the woods and burned them. I stayed until the fire was out. I didn't want the woods to catch on fire."

"We're glad you stayed. That's very responsible. There was also a bird in one of the piles of ashes. Do you know anything about that?"

"No sir. I would never burn an animal. I have burned insects, but Granny says most of them are pests anyway. But she did get on to me for it and said that they have a place in the circle of life. They feed on dead animals and keep the forest clean so it doesn't start stinking."

Lexi let out a small chuckle. "I never thought about it like that, but I bet your grandmother is right. It could be a stinky place if nothing took care of the dead animals."

"That is a good point," John said, "but I have a few more questions and then we'll be done here. There were also some things torn up at the cemetery. We call that vandalism and it's against the law." He paused. "I hate to ask like this, but did you have anything to do with that?"

"No sir. That could make the spirits mad. Granny told me never to make the spirits mad. They deserve to rest in peace, and doing bad things around their graves could make them come after me." He opened his mouth to speak again but closed it and looked down at his hands.

"Is there something you want to tell us?"

"Well, since Charlie explained how these investigations go, and after everything you've told me, do you think all of this stuff has something to do with that lady who was on fire?"

John and Lexi looked at each other. He was a smart kid, but he was too young to be worrying about things like this in life. John took in a deep breath, "That's what we're trying to find out. If you remember seeing anyone at the cemetery who was acting sneaky or anything, it could help us figure out who did all these horrible things."

"I always go there when the cemetery is empty. If I do see someone, even the grounds keeper, I stay in the woods until they go away. Granny taught me how to hide."

John and Lexi sat by the windows after Charlie and Bobby left the office. she looked over at John, he was deep in thought, rubbing his chin like he always did when something bothered him. "He's a good kid. I'm glad he's got someone like Charlie to be friends with."

"Yes, I agree," his voice trailed off.

"So, what's bothering you?"

"I believe the kid was telling the truth. He had nothing to do with any of this, but we're still no closer to figuring this out."

"What about other people at the mining camp? Could someone else from up there be the culprit? The way he talked about his grandmother was kind of creepy."

"Most of them are harmless, quite a bit superstitious though. They believe in a lot of the old ways about spirits and waking the dead. Most of them are terrified of messing with anything like that. Knowing how cultish all of this is going, I can't imagine anyone up there trying to stir up the old spirits, as they call them. I think we're still dealing with one of the town's folks. I just don't know who."

John stood up and returned to his office. Lexi went to her desk and pulled out the old files she'd been going through, thought about everything that was discussed at her Grams' house the night before with some of the older town's people. Nothing was making sense or coming together. She'd been through the files so much she felt like she knew them word for word.

The pyro, who they now knew as Bobby, had been marked off the suspect list. Dell Chimay had a good alibi and couldn't have been involved. Who did that leave?

She sent a group text to Jake, Peyton and Charlie to ask if they were ready for an adventure. It was time they checked out the old hidden estate.

Chapter 25

They decided to meet up for lunch and make their way through the woods to the overgrown estate. As they walked through the woods, Lexi thought about the trails close to her Grams' house that Peyton and she had explored as children, the same trails where she'd found the bodies of an elderly couple right after she moved back to Cryptic Cove. So much had happened in the short time since then. It hadn't been quite two years, but she'd been involved in her share of strange investigations.

As they neared a section of thick woods, the hairs on Lexi's body started to stand on end. Chills and shivers shot through her. They were sure this place had belonged to one of her ancestors, but still had no clue why the whole town had tried to wipe out any information of his existence. She didn't know if that's what bothered her or just the fact that they were about to sneak into an old estate. It reminded her of the old teen mysteries she'd read when as a kid.

Jake reached over and took her hand as they continued to walk. He always had a way of knowing when she needed extra support, when things just didn't feel quite right to her.

They made their way through a thick patch of undergrowth. Luckily, Charlie had brought a machete to chop a way through the forest. They heard a noise and looked up to see a black mass approaching. Baxter and his friends filled the woods. They were eerily quiet instead of their normal chattery selves. It was creepy, but kind of comforting too, knowing that they were there. Baxter let out a caw and then flew towards the estate, guiding their way.

Once they made their way through the last bit of undergrowth, they were on the main property. Even though it had grown up and not been cared for, they stood and admired how beautiful it must have been at one time. Moss covered most of the outbuildings, making them blend into the surrounding woods. It was a wonder the place could even still be seen from the air.

As they approached the main doors to the home, Jake noticed one of them was slightly ajar. He inspected it and assured everyone it had been like that for years. That was a relief. For one thing, they didn't have to break in, but it was also a relief knowing that no one else had been out there snooping around recently. If this estate had anything to do with town secrets and the item Shirley had had in her possession, it was likely the killer was looking for it too, if he was even aware of its existence. Jake opened the door and stepped inside. Charlie rummaged through his backpack and pulled out several flashlights. "Good thinking. I can't believe I left mine in the car." Lexi said as she took one of the lights.

Charlie laughed, "I've been exploring more than you guys. I try to prepare for dark places."

The main entrance was dark, but huge and open. Some natural light came in through the windows. It reminded Lexi of mansions she'd seen in old movies, complete with a gigantic double staircase that led up to the second floor. They decided to stick together, since it was their first time going inside, and to remain on the first floor.

Everything in the home was still intact, albeit covered with dirt and years of grime. There were also bird and bat droppings in several areas indicating that wildlife had used the place as a refuge. That also meant they needed to watch out for snakes. The fall temperatures were much cooler, but that didn't mean they had all gone into hibernation, and with an infestation of rats, it could be a regular buffet for snakes to find their meals.

The kitchen was located at the back of the house. Pots and pans were still on the countertops, like someone had been in the process of cooking a meal and then just disappeared. There was a small staircase, just off the kitchen that led up to the second floor. Probably intended for the kitchen staff, so they didn't have to haul food through the foyer to the main staircase. Under the staircase, tucked into a small alcove in the corner, was a small door, most likely a storage space. Lexi turned to everyone, "This is odd. This door has a really old lock on it. It looks almost like the Cryptex."

Charlie pulled out a rag and began wiping the grime off of the old lock. They stared at it in silence for a few seconds before Peyton finally spoke. "That's the same markings we've found in those files and on the Cryptex."

Lexi's phone beeped. She let out a laugh as a way to break the tension, and pulled the phone out to look at the screen. She stopped laughing when she read the message. "Grams is missing. We need to get back to town."

Chapter 26

Lexi and Peyton headed straight to Crystal Scents. John was still there with Ms. Jensen. "What happened?" She asked as she closed the door behind her.

Ms. Jensen came over and took one of her hands. "Oh dear. I don't even know. She got a phone call and said she had to leave, but she wouldn't tell me who it was or what it was about. I didn't ask too much. I mean, she gets calls all the time and leaves the shop. That was hours ago and now no one knows where she's at. That's just not like her. She's never gone for more than an hour, and if she is, she always calls and lets me know."

Lexi led the distraught woman over to the sofa. "Ms. Jensen, have a seat. I'm sure it's all going to be okay. We will find her. She's stubborn and resourceful."

"I know she is, but I can't shake the feeling that this has something to do with Shirley's death and that awful thing she had hidden all these years. I can't figure out why they'd take Velda though. She doesn't know anything. Well not any more than the rest of us."

Lexi looked up at John. A look of anguish was written across his face. She had a feeling he knew Ms. Jensen was right about Grams being taken because of the Cryptex. She also had the strange feeling that he'd given it to her for safe keeping. If that was true, she hadn't been safe at all. Who would know she had it? She thought back to the night of the meeting at Grams' house. Most of the original descendants were there. They all knew about the object now, and they all knew someone was searching for old town secrets. It had to be one of them. But who?

Lexi knew she and John had to speak privately so she asked Peyton to stay with Ms. Jensen while they went to the office to check on some things.

Jake said he'd start making phone calls to see if anyone he knew had seen Grams. Charlie told Peyton he would go wait for Paisley to get out of school and then bring her into town.

John and Lexi arrived at the office and noticed a piece of paper taped to the door. That wasn't unusual. A lot of times people would leave notes about picking up some produce or they stopped by to leave some goodies. Lexi pulled the note off the door and tucked it under her arm so she could unlock the door.

John went straight to the coffee machine. He normally didn't have coffee this late in the day, but he was upset. Lexi didn't want him to feel like she was on the attack, but she had to ask him some questions. "John, does Grams have the Cryptex? Is that where you went that day, to give it to her?"

He turned around slowly. "Yes. I knew she would keep it safe. Unfortunately, I didn't know it would put her in danger. No one else knows she has it."

"Well, we don't know if she's in danger. There could be a logical explanation for her disappearance. Maybe her cell phone is dead." Lexi said as she opened the note that had been tucked under her arm.

"I hope you're right. We're old and forget to charge all of these new fangled devices."

Lexi's heart sank looking at the note. She sat down in a chair and stared at the words. "Well, we're both wrong. The killer does have her and demands we give them the Cryptex in exchange for Grams."

John rushed over and looked at the note. "My heavens. This can't be happening."

"Well, I suggest we give it to them."

"I don't know where it is, and your grandmother would die before she let such a heinous person have those secrets."

"That's what I'm afraid of. And without that cursed thing, we have no leverage. We can't give them what we don't have."

"I'll go call the sheriff. We need to report this."

Movement at the window caught Lexi's attention. She looked up to see Bobby peeking inside. She waved at him and tried her best to smile. She didn't want him to feel unwelcome, knowing he wasn't used to being around so many new people, but her heart was aching for her grandmother, and her mind was racing with what to do. He had an inquisitive look on his face, so she motioned for him to come on in.

He slowly walked to the door and pulled it open. "Hey there." Lexi said as he stepped through the door. "Is something wrong?"

He opened his jacket and pulled some books out. "I don't know if you can use these. They belong to my Nanna, and she'd have my hide if'n she knew I took them, but the markings on the outside look like the ones I saw on your desk that day I was in here with Charlie." He walked over to the desk and laid them in front of Lexi. They were extremely old. The leather was dried and cracking, but he was right, she could make out some of the symbols on the cover. She opened the book on top, the first entries were dated from the middle 1700s. Cryptic Cove had been established by then and was over fifty years old. She skimmed a few pages until she ran across the name Danforth and stopped to read the entries in detail. The Danforth who'd helped to build Cryptic Cove had been the son of the Danforth who'd played a huge role in the Salem Witch Trials. Unfortunately, he'd been accused of practicing black magic. The town had rebelled against him.

She glanced up at Bobby, who was still standing in front of the desk. "Can you leave these with me, or do you need to get them back to your Nanna."

"Well," he took in a breath, "She would be mad, but if I explain to her that you're fighting a bad guy she might understand."

"I don't want you to get in trouble." A thought popped into her head. "I know what we can do. Since Charlie knows the people up there at the camp, I can have him visit your Nanna and go through these with her. She may know some more of the backstory. How's that sound?"

"I like that idea. My Nanna sure likes Charlie. I think she'd be okay with that."

"That sounds like a plan. But, before you go, would you like a cup of hot chocolate, and maybe a donut?"

"Yes ma'am, that would be great."

She fixed him a cup of cocoa to go and a little goodie bag. As soon as he left, she called Peyton and explained what she had read in the old journals from the mining town. It didn't help her find Grams or give any clue as to who had taken her, but at least now they knew what the killer may be after…an old man's black magic.

Chapter 27

John was beside himself with worry. For the first time since she'd met him and been reunited with her family, she saw how much he loved her. He would never overstep his boundary and still had great respect for Lexi's late grandfather, but there was no denying he was in love with her grandmother.

Lexi told him to go to Grams' house and wait by the phone there, in case the kidnapper called to make an exchange. He wasn't much use to her in his present state of mind. He was trying to hold it together and had always been a rock of reserve in this town, but this hurt him deeply.

She called Jake and explained everything to him. He was tied up with some insurance matters, but would be by as soon as he was done. Lexi wracked her brain and knew she couldn't just sit around and do nothing, so she headed down to the Magistrate's office to talk to Mavis Clark. She used to be one of the last people Lexi even wanted to speak to, but she knew Mavis loved this town, was aware of the old town secrets and had made amends with Grams. In a strange way, they had become close friends. With new information about the estate and the Danforth who had lived there, maybe she could put two and two together. At least she'd have a new starting point of where to look into town records and old real estate papers. Luckily, Lexi had photocopied a few pages from the journals little Bobby had shown her, so they had some reference points.

One name kept popping up, but they couldn't pinpoint it to anyone in town. Lexi thanked Mavis for her time and headed back to the office to wait on Jake. While she waited, she decided to check some of her old skip-trace resources for old medical records, marriage records, whatever she could find. Once again it felt like grasping at straws.

She typed in the name Osborne, the one that had been in the town records but disappeared after a certain date. She assumed they'd all died off without any children or family members. As she started reading through some of the files, something dawned on her. They were driven out of Cryptic Cove.

She kept going through file after file until finally, Bingo! There was the missing link. Her heart jolted. She couldn't believe who the descendent was. It wasn't one of their suspects, but the more she thought about it, the more sense it made.

She grabbed the phone and made a quick call to Marcus Finche, the town coroner and amateur forensics guy. She asked him to look at some specific files and get back with her. In the meantime, she was headed out to confront the person she believed was the Danforth descendent. She couldn't imagine why anyone would want to dig up such horrible things from the past. On the other hand, she didn't really want to know how someone could be so evil. All she wanted was to get Grams back safely and put this crazy mess behind them. She still had a wedding to plan, although at this point, it looked like it would be postponed indefinitely.

Chapter 28

Lexi headed to the library knowing it would be closed, but her gut told her there were secrets still hidden in some of those files, and she intended to find out what they were. Breaking and entering wasn't the right thing to do, but sometimes, in dire circumstances, it was necessary.

She pulled around to the back of the library and saw Ms. Jensen approaching the back door. She quickly got out of her car and walked towards her. The older woman spun around, a look of guilt on her face. "Ms. Jensen, what are you doing here?" Lexi asked.

She stammered her words out, "I— well." In a moment of defiance, she raised her head and looked Lexi square in the eyes. "There are files still in the library, some I didn't take before my retirement. I know they contain secrets and I intend to find them."

"I'm here for the same reason. It's illegal for us to break in. I'm willing to take the chance and get in trouble for it, but you don't need to be involved in it. Let me do this, okay?"

She pulled her hand out of her pocket and jangled a key, "Oh, there's no need to break in. I still have a key." A mischievous glint lit up her eyes.

"Ms. Jensen, I never would have pegged you for the type to keep something like that."

"Well, I have some of that intuition stuff too. Something told me a long time ago that I needed to have access."

"Then let's get in there and find those files." Lexi held her flashlight up. "I have my flashlight. It's come in handy a lot in my life."

"Wow, that looks nice and sturdy."

"John gave it to me when I started working for him."

"Is that the one you conked ole Bernie Copeland with?"

"It is."

"I'm glad you have it. There should be some light from the windows still shining into the basement, but it won't be much. I think I know exactly where to look, if Decatur hasn't discovered where I had some of the files stashed. There shouldn't have been any need for her to go into the old basement."

Ms. Jensen unlocked the door and they quickly stepped inside. Lexi didn't want to tell her that she had doubts about Mrs. Williams not rummaging through the whole library, so she didn't say anything. She clicked on the flashlight so they could see their way down the dark hall with Ms. Jensen leading the way. She stopped in front of an old door. "This is it. This thing used to stick so bad. I bet it's even worse now."

Lexi stepped up, "Let me do it then." She grabbed the knob, turned it and gave it a good shove, almost falling when it flung open like it had been greased. "Oh crap!" She gasped, louder than she intended. She looked back at Ms. Jensen. "Apparently it's been fixed."

Ms. Jensen walked through the open door and started heading down the stairs. "That means she's been down here snooping around. Shine the light for me. I'm not as young as I used to be."

Lexi shined the light down the stairs and followed behind her. Suddenly she stopped. "Do you hear that? It sounds like someone shuffling around."

Lexi listened and heard it, too. She pulled out the taser gun that Jake had gotten her. "Let me go first. I don't want you getting hurt."

Ms. Jensen smiled looking at the taser. "You come prepared."

"Not as prepared as I should be." Lexi told her, knowing she should stop and call John to come check this out, but since she was already there, she might as well do it. It was probably a rat anyway. A big rat, by the sounds of it.

They eased their way down. The noise stopped. Ms. Jensen pointed to the direction she last heard the noise. They reached the bottom of the stairs and Lexi pointed the light towards where her companion was pointing. Ms. Jensen gasped when she saw the face. She rushed past Lexi. "Oh my lands, Velda. Who on earth has tied you up down here? We've been so worried about you. Thank God you're alright." She said as she pulled the gag away from Grams' mouth.

"That woman is completely crazy!" Grams spat the words out, exasperated.

They began untying her. "Who did this, Grams?" Lexi asked as she got the last of the ropes loose.

"Decatur Williams. And when I get my hands on her, I'm going to wring her scrawny little neck!"

"Where is she now?"

Grams smoothed back her hair, always concerned about her appearance. "She's headed to the house, to get that Cryptex. I didn't want to tell her where it was, but she threatened to hurt everyone I love. I couldn't take the chance, so I told her I had it hidden, hoping she'd go look and give me a chance to escape. She's crazy as a loon and just as dangerous as she is nuts."

"It's okay Grams. John is there, in case the kidnapper called your home phone."

"We have to get to him. She will kill him if she doesn't get that cursed contraption. She's already killed two people over it, Lexi. We have to get to John."

"I'll go, you stay with Ms. Jensen I can call John on my way and warn him."

They all headed up the stairs as Lexi pulled out her cellphone. Decatur already had a good head start. The phone rang several times before going to voicemail. Lexi pushed the end button and then punched the quick dial for Jake. Hopefully, he could get there before she did. She prayed it wasn't too late.

* * *

As Lexi pulled into the driveway everything seemed ominous and quiet. She parked the car and went around to the backdoor. When she entered the kitchen, she could hear someone rummaging through another room, throwing things around. She saw John lying on the floor with several large drops of blood next to his head. She eased over and checked his pulse. He was still alive. She listened to the sound of the ransacking to determine which room the noise was coming from. If she could sneak in, she might be able to attack from behind. She sucked in a deep breath and headed towards the living room. She peeked in and saw Decatur Williams yanking books from the bookshelf, muttering under her breath. If she could just make it across the room before the woman turned around and spotted her, she could tackle her like a linebacker would in a football game.

She slowly made her way into the room, creeping quietly. Halfway to the woman, she took a step and heard a loud creak. *Crap!* She muttered to herself. She forgot about the one creaky floorboard in Grams' house. Decatur turned around and spotted her. Lexi almost froze in her steps, but instead, rushed forward. The thought of tackling an old woman caused her heart to pinch, but it had to be done before the woman killed anyone else or unleashed any evil she'd find in that old estate if she discovered where the Cryptex was.

The woman side-stepped as Lexi tripped over books lying on the floor, falling towards the bookshelf. She pulled her hands up and caught herself. Mrs. Williams grabbed a large book and smacked Lexi over the back of the head. "Why are you trying to stop me? You're a Danforth. We could run this town together! Don't you want to reclaim what is rightfully ours?"

Lexi fell to the floor and quickly turned over, trying to get to her feet again. She looked up and saw the giant book coming towards her face. "You're crazy lady! I have no intention of trying to unleash anything evil on this town." She raised her leg and kicked the woman in the knee, a move Jake had taught her during their self-defense classes. The woman screamed in pain, but raised the book again.

Lexi heard a loud caw as Baxter and several other crows flew into the room and began swooping down, pecking the woman on the head with each pass. "Get off me you crazy birds. I've had enough of your kind pecking me." She yelled as she tried to swing the book at them. They swooped and dodged her attempts to hit them.

Lexi got to her feet and spotted one of Grams' table runners on the floor. It was long and hopefully thin enough to use as a rope. She grabbed it and flung it around the woman. With a quick jerk to her left she pulled the woman off her feet. The woman hit the floor with a thud. Lexi quickly sat on top of her, trying to wrangle the table runner around her. It wasn't the best thing to use as a rope, but it did help.

Jake rushed into the room. "Lexi! Are you okay?"

"I'm okay. Help me tie this crazy woman up."

Jake stepped over the piles of books on the floor and grabbed Decatur's hands. "There's some handcuffs in my back pocket." He said to Lexi. "Get them out and put them on her."

Lexi reached around to Jake's back pocket and pulled out the handcuffs. The woman kept fighting, but Lexi finally got her hands bound.

They got her to her feet and headed to the front door. John was sitting on the steps holding a rag to the gash on his head, just as Grams and Ms. Jensen came barreling into the driveway. Grams' car came to a screeching halt, kicking up dust when a tire left the pavement. Grams jumped out and ran to John. *She's very spry for her age*, Lexi thought as her Grams ran straight for John and threw her arms around his neck. He had a good gash across his forehead, but relief washed over his face as he rubbed her back. It was clear that they did have feelings for each other. Maybe now they would stop trying to hide it from everyone, and just be together. There was nothing wrong with people their age becoming a couple. Maybe a marriage would be in their future too.

Ms. Jensen got out of the car, walked up to Decatur Williams and poked her in the chest. "You've got some nerve trying to pull a stunt like this on our town. I'm sure you don't have the decency to be ashamed of yourself, but you should be."

Decatur puffed up and started to speak just as Ms. Jensen shoved her scarf into the old ladies mouth. "Stuff it you crazy old bat. We don't want to hear a thing you have to say. You can tell the judge your pathetic story."

Jake grinned and shook his head as he grabbed Lexi's hand and pulled her towards him and kissed her on the forehead. "You just can't stay out of trouble, can you?"

Lexi started to speak but looked up and saw the playful smile on his face. "I guess I can't."

He pulled Lexi into a hug as they both looked over towards the porch. Grams was doting on John and inspecting the gash on his forehead. She looked at Lexi, "I don't think it needs stitches, but it does need one of those butterfly bandages. Lexi would you grab the first aid kit?"

"Yes ma'am," She said as she let go of Jake and headed into the house to grab the kit. She glanced into the living room on her way to the kitchen. She didn't have time to think about how bad things could have been. She didn't like seeing Grams' home in such a mess, but she shook the thought off and hurried past the living room straight for the kitchen to grab Grams' bag of first aid items. By the time she got back outside, the sheriff was there, loading Mrs. Williams into the back of his car. She was still struggling and would have been screaming if it wasn't for the scarf still stuck in her mouth. Lexi giggled thinking the sheriff didn't want to listen to her either, since he made no effort to remove it.

Another murder was solved, but there was still so much she didn't know. She was ready to put the madness behind them. She looked at Jake and thought about wedding plans.

Chapter 29

Even though John didn't need stitches, Grams insisted he go to the hospital, in case he had a concussion. He opened his mouth to argue, but thought better of it. The worry in Grams' eyes softened his heart.

Jake excused himself as Lexi and Grams got John checked in, and by the time he was settled into his room, all of their friends were there. Jake came in with a man Lexi didn't recognize, although most everyone else knew him. He stepped up and took Lexi's hands as he looked into her eyes. The room grew noticeably quiet, so she looked around and saw that everyone was staring at her. "What's going on Jake?" She whispered.

That infectious smile that she fell in love with, and still fell in love with every time she saw it, swept across his face. "I want to get married."

She let out a soft giggle. "I know. We've been trying to plan a wedding, remember."

"I don't want to wait. I want to marry you right now, right here. That's why all of our friends are here."

"Oh? I wondered why they all showed up so quickly. You sneaky thing. You planned all of this didn't you?"

"Well, I didn't plan John getting hit over the head, but it seems like the perfect time to get married."

Bobby and Paisley stepped up to announce they were the ring-bearer and flower girl, Peyton stepped in as maid of honor, of course, and Charlie was the best man. Lexi turned to look at John, one of the most treasured men in her life. It was only fitting that he give her away. He blushed and tears rolled down his cheeks. "Oh you sweet girl, I'd be honored."

After they said I-Dos and everyone got a cupcake that Peyton had brought, Lexi looked at Jake, tears in her eyes. She couldn't believe he was now her husband, or that she was a wife. A real wife. He pulled her close, and she snuggled in under his arm.

She looked around the room at her big family. These people were more than just friends, they were a part of who she was becoming. She finally had a real family. She missed her mom and dad, and she was still upset at all they'd hidden from her, but having all these people around her helped her get through it. She glanced over in the corner of the room where Charlie and Peyton were standing with Bobby and Paisley. It suddenly dawned on her that they were the perfect family. She nudged Jake to look over their way. He leaned into her ear. "Maybe you'll get to plan a wedding after all."

"I hope so. I know Peyton is still bothered by the incident a few months ago, but Charlie has really stepped in and helped her heal a lot."

Lexi took in a deep breath. It was good to know that she and Peyton both had these people, and they could heal from all the past hurts surrounded by those who loved them.

Chapter 30

The next day, Ms. Jensen gave Lexi the old files she'd taken from the library before her retirement several years ago. Mostly old documents on how the forefathers had established the town after fleeing from Salem in the 1690s. None of them were clear about whether or not the early settlers were actually witches, or just disagreed with the whole witch trial ordeal and didn't want any part of it.

Close to the bottom of the stack, Lexi found a file that mentioned a Danforth. He had been extremely wealthy and had a big part of setting the town up. He'd built a large estate on the outskirts of town. By the early 1700s, he'd fallen out of favor with the town's people. She continued to read the story.

A notation in the margin close to the bottom of the page caught her eye. They had left Salem because of the burning of those accused of witchcraft, but had found themselves in a similar situation when they discovered that Danforth was practicing black magic. They'd raided his home, dragged him into the center of town and burned him alive. Afterwards, they'd made a pact to hide all evidence of his existence from the generations that followed.

Charlie had opened the Cryptex. It took him several hours to figure out the code, but he finally cracked it. Inside was an old key. The key must be important, but no one had a clue what door it would unlock or where the door was. It could be any old building in town, or any back room in the old buildings. Unfortunately, it was still a mystery, but at least they knew who killed Shirley and the woman would be brought to justice.

Lexi couldn't believe that someone could hold a grudge as long as Decatur had. It had been hundreds of years ago when her ancestors set out to destroy anyone they thought was practicing witchcraft, but they'd had a traitor in their midst. Unfortunately, Decatur followed the life of the traitor. So many innocent people died back then. She couldn't wrap her head around the fact that someone in this day and time had been burned to death because of witchcraft. It didn't matter that the town's people of today weren't practicing the craft, and no one could be sure that their ancestors had either, although it did seem plausible. The early settlers fled Salem for a reason, and kept many secrets, some of which were still hidden today.

The whole truth may never be known, but it was true that many of the descendants of those early town builders did have special gifts, the gift of insight or intuitions. Lexi herself had little gut feelings that weren't like normal gut feelings, and she dreamed of ghosts. She let out a long breath. She had absolutely no intention of trying to speak to the dead on purpose, but like finding dead bodies, if it happened that way, so be it.

The older town's folk decided it was time to turn things over to the younger bunch. Discovering the mystery of the key would be interesting and keep them busy. Lexi and Peyton loved snooping into things. As the new secret keepers of the town, they decided there would be no secrets. Whatever they discovered would become town knowledge, even if the past was full of horrible things no one wanted to hear about. It was best to get things out in the open and hopefully avoid future revenge from Salem's descendants. Since there had been one out there, there could be others, still digging and clinging to those old witch hunts. Some people held on to the past without learning from it.

John decided to step down as town constable and leave Jake as the appointed official. Lexi was excited for Jake and his new position, although she had her doubts about them spending all their time together at home and at work. How would she handle Jake being her husband *and* her boss.

A Note From the Author

I strive to bring you enjoyable stories with characters you'll love. I hope you've enjoyed this short mystery. Although each book goes through several rounds of edits and through several grammar and style checkers, sometimes we miss things—we are all human. If you find any glaring mistakes, please let us know so we can get them fixed and our files updated. Thank you.

Be sure to check out more of my cozy mysteries. You can find a listing at the back of this book.

About the Author

K.P. Stafford is a Mom, Nana and Musician's wife!

She's been writing crazy bits and pieces most of her life. In 2016, she took the plunge to become a full-time fiction author.

When she's not writing, she's thinking up things to write about, spending time with her family and sometimes she just relaxes.

In a name–Vincent Price!

That's who started her on this road of wanting to be a writer—and lover of all things creepy and spooky and haunted–although she doesn't necessarily write haunted tales.

www.kpstafford.com

Also by K.P. Stafford

Cryptic Cove Cozy Mystery Series:

Murder and Mayhem - A Cryptic Cove Cozy Mystery (Book 1)

Murder and Menace - A Cryptic Cove Cozy Mystery (Book 2)

Murder & Mockery - A Cryptic Cove Cozy Mystery (Book 3)

Murder & Marriage - A Cryptic Cove Cozy Mystery (Book 4 - coming in 2020)

Mystery Theater Presents Cozy Mystery Series

Mrs. Pickles Perilous Parting - A Mystery Theater Presents Cozy Mystery

Preview: Mrs. Pickles Perilous Parting

Mrs. Pickles Perilous Parting - A Mystery Theater Presents Cozy Mystery
Chapter One

"Cut!" Yelled Lewis Marble. "This is unacceptable! How can any of you call this acting? It's absolutely atrocious."

The cast on stage turned to look at him as he threw the manuscript down and stomped off towards the side door.

He almost plowed into Jess as she entered to see what all the commotion was about. The crew on stage bickered among themselves.

"Clara, I told you to work on that line. You miss it every time and Lewis throws a fit. If you can't do any better than this, quit." Carter Stewart, the lead man in the production, told her through clenched teeth.

Clara's large chest heaved under the tight fabric of her costume and looked like it would rip at any minute from the pressure. Redness crept up from her neck to her face. Her breath was ragged, "That man is an idiot. You know good and well I am doing the line in a much better manner than he wants it done. I know this story inside and out and have seen it performed live on several occasions. The way I'm doing it works better." She grabbed at her chest before storming off backstage. She was aware the costume was too tight on her, but she refused to let the alteration lady let it out. She'd been saying for weeks she'd just lose a few pounds and it'd be fine. But, with the number of dessert cakes she shoved into her mouth, everyone knew it wouldn't happen.

Carter Stewart turned to face Jessica, "The woman is insane. There's no way this will be ready for a live performance in two weeks if she keeps botching the lines and missing her cues. It's pathetic. We need to replace her before she ruins the whole production."

"It's two weeks to opening night. There's no way we can recast her part this late in the game." Jess said.

"Rosie can step in and do it." Carter rebuked.

Jess shook her head. "I don't want to take the risk. Clara is just having a bad day."

Carter rubbed the back of his neck and let out an audible sigh, "She has a bad day, every day. Why don't you see it and do something about it?" He turned and stormed off backstage as Clara had done.

Jessica looked at the remaining crew and told them rehearsal was over for the day.

Lewis returned and stomped up behind her, "I haven't called it a day. Rehearsal isn't over until I say it's over. I'm the director of this fiasco you call an acting crew."

Jess whirled around, staring him in the eyes. "Well, as the owner of this theater," she whirled her hands in the air, "I'm pulling rank and calling it a night. Since I have the keys to the place, it's locked up when I say it is. I suggest you go home, have a drink or whatever and come back fresh tomorrow."

His nostrils flared and a whoosh sound escaped them. Jess prepared herself for the backlash, but fortunately, he complied and stormed off, again. It had been one of the most trying days of her life since taking over the small community theater. A niggling in her gut told her the madness was just starting.

* * *

Two weeks away from pulling off the largest production Jessica had taken on since the death of her parents, Henry and Mary James. Everything that could go wrong had gone wrong, almost all in one day. Nerves were on edge, the stage cast kept missing cues. Today was a dress rehearsal, as they called it. The costume designer was in a frenzy to see how the costumes moved and flowed before she did final alterations. Sound problems, set problems, actor problems and a whole list of other problems that could make or break this show and her little theater.

At 9:00 pm Jess did her nightly rounds, making sure everything was secure and ready to go for the following day. She'd dealt with complaints from everyone and she was ready to get home to her best companion, her cat.

Jess wearily walked down the main hallway, glancing at the photos enshrined to those who had made it on to bigger and better stages, and the ones who'd passed on before their time. Her parent's photo hung as the newest entry. They had made it to Broadway, but after a few years of the hustle, they'd purchased the small, run-down theater and settled in Peculiar. It had only been two years since their deaths. In that time, Jess had put on several small productions that covered some of the expenses, but this was the largest undertaking she'd had the courage to tackle. Times seemed so much easier when she was growing up in the theater. Actors and stagehands were different when she was a kid. Everyone was like family. Some of them stayed on to help her, but others had decided it was time to call it quits. Her parents were the glue that held everyone together. There was no way she could ever take their place, and it showed in the attitudes of several of the cast and crew members. If this production wasn't a success, she had no clue how many would stick out the struggles with her and try to get this theater back on solid ground. Local enthusiasm showed interest when they announced the production several months back, but that didn't always mean it would be a success. The closer it got to curtain-call, the more everyone's nerves were on edge. It was just par for the course.

* * *

Carter Stewart, who was playing the second leading role, had grated on her nerves most of the day. He was one who was sure he'd make it to Broadway. He'd had several auditions and somehow he thought it gave him authority and made him a slice above the rest. He could be a pain to work with. Today was no exception. Clara Stiles, the leading lady was off her game and kept messing up her lines. Carter's patience wore thin because he knew everyone's lines in the whole performance. His arrogance never helped matters, but since he was a good actor, most people overlooked his eccentric nature.

Jess let out a long sigh, sometimes she loved the quietness in the theater at the end of a long day. She enjoyed the alone time after everyone had gone home. Well, almost everyone. The resident ghost,

Farley, was always around, somewhere. He loved to play pranks on Jess when she was there alone. After growing up around him, she'd gotten used to it. As she neared the end of the hall, she half expected him to come flying out of a wall. Secretly, she hoped he was as tired as everyone else and would leave her be tonight.

She checked the doors and lights, making sure everything was secure and in place for tomorrow's whirlwind of pre-production chaos. She looked up to see Farley floating beside her. He took the recognition as his cue to jabber on about how Clara Stiles kept missing her lines and how the new girl, Rosie Peabody, was more suited to the part. Jess drew in a breath and let it out. "It's been a tiring day, Farley. Not only with all the problems, which I'm sure you're aware of, but I had to listen to Becky go on and on about some hot, gorgeous guy at the coffee shop." She emphasized the words hot and gorgeous. Her and Becky's taste in men were usually the complete opposite, so she wasn't amused hearing about Becky's latest find, especially considering she had eyed the guy and thought he'd be perfect for Jess.

She was in no mood to be setup on a blind date…or any kind of date, for that matter. "I don't need this tonight. Okay?"

"Yes, how rude of me." He pouted, "But, I've had no one to talk to all day. You've been busy."

"I'm sorry, Farley. You know how hectic it is the last few weeks before a production goes live. I'm well aware that everything is falling apart. I'm well aware that if I don't pull this off, everything I've known and loved my whole life is down the drain."

She was one of the few people Farley would have a conversation with, but she wasn't excited about that fact tonight. He spent his time making ghostly noises so everyone knew the small theater in Peculiar, Connecticut was, in fact, haunted. He'd been an actor himself and died in the theater when he fell from the stage. She was a small child at the time and he doted on her, but showbiz was his life. It still was, even after his death.

"Oh yes. I so miss the hub-bub of it all. It's not quite the same since I'm dead. And you are correct, this production is a make it or break it one. All the reason you should listen to me about these so-called actors not doing their parts right. I've heard Rosie practice. She's not bad."

Jess looked at Farley and shook her head in disbelief as she opened the door to Clara's dressing room and peeked in. A pile of clothing in the middle of the floor caught her attention. She walked through the doorway, with Farley still yakking. Stopping in her tracks she let out a gasp, her hands flew to cover her mouth. Farley stopped his complaining and fell silent as Jess ran to the woman lying on the floor.

"Clara, are you okay?" she asked.

Farley floated over her and looked down at her, "She's dead."

Jess looked up at him, "Call nine one one."

"Oh yes, where did I leave my cell phone?" he said as he ran his hands through his semi-invisible body. "It must be in my other body."

Jess looked up at him, eyes wide, "Oh, yeah. I'll call them. Maybe they can save her."

"My dear child, the woman is dead."

"How can you be sure? Are you a doctor?"

"I'm a ghost. I know dead when I see it."

Sadness fell over Jess' face. He had a point. She looked down at the body and stuck her fingers under the woman's scarf, anyway. A chill ran through her body at the feel of the cool, clammy skin. Now that her eyes had adjusted to the low lighting, Jess could tell the woman had already taken on a grey hue. With her head bowed she whispered a small prayer before standing up. After she left the room and pulled the door shut, she leaned against the wall. *This can't be happening.* Every ounce of energy had left her body, but she knew she had to report it. She pulled out her cell phone, took a deep, ragged breath and punched in nine-one-one.

Farley stuck his head through the wall as Jess hung up the phone with the emergency response people. "I guess Rosie will get the part now. I hope she's ready to perform in two weeks."

Jess put her hands on her hips and gave Farley the evil eye. "Do you have to be so insensitive?"

He tapped his ethereal temple, "I'm dead. I'm supposed to be insensitive."

Jess blew her hair out of her face and turned to walk down the hall to wait on the police to arrive. The door opened as she approached it. Her assistant, Becky Collins, walked in, jabbering on about how she forgot to take the mail with her, but stopped and stared into Jess' eyes when she noticed something wasn't right.

"What's wrong. You don't look so good."

Jess sat down in a chair, her knees shaking and her resolve failing. She tried to keep it together, but everything was crashing down around her. She finally spoke as Becky walked over to the chair beside her. "Clara's dead. I found her in the dressing room."

Becky stopped in her tracks, her hands went to her mouth. "Oh, my gosh. What happened?" She asked as she slunk down on the seat next to Jess and placed her hands on Jess' knee.

"I'm not sure. I found her on the floor when I went to check the room and she was just dead."

"A heart attack, maybe?"

"Could be. She was off the mark on all of her lines today. We all assumed it was because her costume was too tight and distracting her. Maybe she was sick?"

Farley chimed in, "Maybe the costume smothered her to death."

Becky glared into the ghostly mist beside Jess. Her mouth opened to speak. Jess raised a hand, "This isn't the time to argue with a ghost."

Farley stuck his nose in the air and floated off.

Becky and Jess sat in silence waiting for the police to arrive. Jess was glad to have her best friend with her. She didn't want to think selfishly at a time like this but losing her leading lady two weeks before the show could cause her to lose everything. She wasn't sure how she would pull out of this mess. She took in a deep breath and tried to be thankful she was alive. Clara sure hadn't been so lucky.

Made in United States
North Haven, CT
20 October 2023

42983623R00104